Lisa

Beach Brides Series

by

Denise Devine

Love, Laughter and happily ever after!

Denise Devine

Lisa

Beach Brides Series

Copyright 2017 by Denise Devine

www.deniseannettedevine.com

ISBN: 978-1-943124-01-5

Published in the United States of America.

Edited by L. F. Nies and J. Dalton

Cover design by Raine English
Elusive Dreams Designs
www.ElusiveDreamsDesigns.com

Dedication

To my sister, Lisa Kay, the inspiration for this book.
And in memory of my cousin, Shelby.

Introduction

GRAB YOUR BEACH hat and a towel and prepare for a brand-new series brought to you by twelve New York Times and USA Today bestselling authors...

Beach Brides! Fun in the summer sun!

Twelve heartwarming, sweet novellas linked by a unifying theme. You'll want to read each one!

BEACH BRIDES SERIES (Lisa)

Twelve friends from the online group, Romantic Hearts Book Club, decide to finally meet in person during a destination vacation to beautiful Enchanted Island. While of different ages and stages in life, these ladies have two things in common: 1) they're diehard romantics, and 2) they've been let down by love. As a wildly silly dare during her last night on the island, each heroine decides to stuff a note in a bottle addressed to her "dream hero" and cast it out to sea! Sending a message in a bottle can't be any crazier than online or cell phone dating, or posting personal ads! And, who knows? One of these mysterious missives might actually lead to love...

Join Meg, Tara, Nina, Clair, Jenny, Lisa, Hope, Kim, Rose, Lily, Faith and Amy as they embark on the challenge of a lifetime: risking their hearts to accomplish their dreams.

This is Lisa's story...

When Lisa Kaye loses her job and her boyfriend, she returns to Enchanted Island, the idyllic place of her childhood, and finds true love through a message in a bottle.

Meet all of the Beach Brides!

Meg (Julie Jarnagin)

Tara (Ginny Baird)

Nina (Stacey Joy Netzel)

Clair (Grace Greene)

Jenny (Melissa McClone)

Lisa (Denise Devine)

Hope (Aileen Fish)

Kim (Magdalena Scott)

Rose (Shanna Hatfield)

Lily (Ciara Knight)

Faith (Helen Scott Taylor)

Amy (Raine English)

Excerpt Copyright Information

Prologue and Chapter One from *Hope (Beach Brides Series)* by Aileen Fish

Copyright © 2017 Aileen Fish

Prologue

LISA'S MESSAGE IN a bottle...

To Whom it may concern,

I'm an adventurous girl, who'd love to see the world, but I don't have the money or the time.

If I met someone, though, who liked to travel for fun, he'd become a best friend of mine.

I love the mountains, the seas, the rocks and the trees, and the Cairo Museum of Antiquities.

I've never seen a polar bear, or visited The World's Fair, or climbed the Eiffel Tower in France.

I want to see pyramids, ride a tram atop a rainforest, and visit Spain to watch the Flamenco dance.

Do you like piña coladas and strolling in the rain? Is there a special place in the world you'd love to see again?

If you're a guy who loves to fly, or cruise on the mighty sea, then give me a shout, tell me what you're all about, 'cause you might be the one for me.

IslandGirl#1@...

Chapter One

Enchanted Island, East Caribbean

The Month of July

LISA KAYE SIPPED her wine and stared at the blank page in front of her, wondering how to compose a message to a man she'd never met.

The twelve women in her group, The Romantic Hearts Book Club, had chosen to spend their last night vacationing together on Enchanted Island working on a "spur-of-the-moment" project. The group had read and discussed many romance novels since the club's inception and each woman had a favorite hero from the book of her choice, a man she would love to call her own. Lisa didn't know who had suggested the concept, but after a spirited discussion and a couple rounds of cocktails, the group had concluded that each woman would compose a personal message to her "dream hero," stuff it into a bottle and throw the bottle in the Caribbean ocean. In Lisa's opinion, the chance of anyone—much less the perfect man—finding her bottle and taking the message seriously seemed ludicrous, but everyone else had agreed to do it so she decided to go along with the plan.

After dinner, the women gathered at the poolside bar to take in the balmy air of their last evening together at the Hideaway Cove Resort. The atmosphere vibrated through the open-air pavilion with the jaunty, percussion-like sounds of Reggae music played on steel drums. A small group of people played a lively game of volleyball in the adjacent pool.

Sitting at a round table for two, Lisa rested her hand on her chin and tried to come up with something clever to put in her message. The harder she tried to concentrate, though, the more her mind stubbornly refused to cooperate.

The young woman sitting across from her sipped a glass of Chablis. "How are you doing on your message?" Clair inquired as the warm Caribbean breeze ruffled a few wisps of hair from her French braid. Her dark locks contrasted richly against her magenta sundress. "Are you making any progress?"

Lisa slid the blank paper toward Clair and sighed. "I can't even get started. How are you coming along with yours?"

"I need to work on mine, but I'm not putting a lot of effort into it. I don't see the point in writing a message to a complete stranger when I already have a dream hero back at home." Clair's fine brows drew together in annoyance as she leaned closer. "If you ask me, the idea is pretty silly."

Lisa: Beach Brides Series

Lisa nodded. "It's risky, too. What if the wrong person gets hold of my bottle and begins to stalk me on line?"

Clair's brown eyes widened with an incredulous stare. "You're not going to put your personal email address on it, are you?"

Lisa shook her head. "No way, I've created a new one specifically for this purpose and I'm not using my real name. If anyone replies, I'll know the person found the bottle."

"I did the same thing," Clair replied. "I don't want anyone getting hold of my personal information." She slid the sheet of paper back to Lisa. "Think of your ideal man and write to him."

Lisa chuckled. "As a kid, I had a crush on Indiana Jones. I used to run around the house wearing my dad's Fedora, a brown vest and carrying my sister's lunge whip, pretending that Indy and I were exploring archeological wonders together. I've read quite a few books with that type of character and I've loved them all." She doodled on the paper, drawing a crude outline of a small treasure map. "Sometimes I wish I'd pursued a college degree in archaeology instead of business administration. Maybe I'd be doing something more exciting with my life now instead of supervising the Personal Lines Department of an insurance agency."

Clair grabbed a business card off another table and flipped it over to the blank side. "This will work. Do you have a pen I could borrow?"

She handed Clair a pen and went back to work, racking her brain to come up with something suitable.

After twenty minutes, another glass of wine and three sheets of paper, Lisa showed her message to Clair. "It sounds more like a Dr. Seuss book than a memo to Mr. Right, but that's the best I can do."

Clair picked up the sheet and scanned the words. "It's cute. And totally you. I like it." She slid it back across the table. "What are you using for a bottle?"

"Gosh, I forgot to get one." Lisa began to fold the paper into a narrow strip. "I wonder if I can get a beer bottle and a cork from the bar."

But when she went to the bar and asked for a bottle to use, the bartender refused, warning her that the resort forbade throwing any trash into the bay. She'd purchased an antique bottle from a small curio shop in the island's historic downtown area, but she certainly didn't want to use that one. The cobalt bottle had attracted her, embossed with "Owl Drug Company" and a figure of an owl sitting upon a mortar with one claw clutching the pestle. The shopkeeper had remarked that he came by the bottle after a local resident had fished it out of the bay. She hated the thought of throwing it back in there!

Unless I don't actually toss the bottle—just

make it look like I threw it...

The early evening sun dipped low in the sky, hanging over the endless horizon of the Caribbean ocean like a crimson ball of fire. The twelve women laughed and talked as they walked through a grove of palms in an undeveloped area next to the resort. Tara and Meg led the way along the well-trodden trail to a remote strip of shoreline, far enough from the resort so no one in the area could see them tossing their bottles into the water. Jenny and Faith were next in line. They vowed to organize another group getaway and smacked their palms together in agreement. Behind them, Nina and Hope joined in, laughing as they offered a few suggestions.

Lisa and Clair hung back, trailing the group so they could chat.

"Ouch! Wait a minute." Clair stopped and pulled off one of her silver flip-flops to remove a tiny fragment of coral stuck in the ball of her foot. She looked up. "Are you leaving tomorrow with us or are you staying on to visit with your aunt?"

"I came a few days early and spent time with her," Lisa said as they stood on the sandy trail. "She wants me to move here permanently to take over her bed and breakfast hotel."

Her Aunt Elsie Dubois lived in a large white house with blue trim on the edge of the island's business district. Lisa had poignant childhood memories of time spent here, roaming the

Denise Devine

cobblestone streets of "old town" Morganville and playing on the beaches with her cousins. The thought of living here permanently tugged at her heartstrings, but...

"Are you serious?" Clair slipped her flip-flop back on and resumed walking. "That sounds like a dream come true! Are you considering it?"

Lisa sighed with regret, knowing an opportunity like that would never come along again. "I'd love to accept the offer, but I have too many ties back home to just drop everything and move here." She leaned close to Clair to keep their conversation private. "The last time I talked to my guy on the phone he said he had something important to tell me." She didn't know for sure, but she had the feeling Rob planned to surprise her with an engagement ring. He said he didn't want to talk about it until they were together again. What else could it be? She smiled to herself. The thought of one day becoming Rob Mancuso's wife made her heart brim with hope. "I can't wait to get back to West Palm Beach."

Clair gave her a brief, knowing smile. "I've had a great time here, but I'm getting a little antsy to get home, too."

Though she didn't say any more, Lisa understood that Clair missed the "hero" in her life and wanted to see him again.

They walked out of the palm grove and along the rocky shore until they reached an area that looked suitable to toss their bottles.

"Okay, everyone," Tara said as the group lined up. "On the count of three, throw 'em in."

Claire shook her head and mumbled, "Here goes nothing."

Lisa drew the small blue bottle from her purse that held her message. She stood poised to throw it, but intended to merely go through the motion then quickly slip it back into her purse before anyone noticed.

"One...two...three!"

An assortment of glass in a blend of colors, sizes and shapes flew through the air and dropped into the ocean in a succession of loud plunks and splashes. Lisa clutched her bottle and swung her arm, but the bottle had something slippery on it. The oily liquid squished through her fingers. The cap on the sunscreen lotion she carried in her purse must have loosened and leaked all over everything. Darn! The bottle suddenly flew from her hand and sailed through the air like a missile then disappeared into the water, leaving only a circular wave of ripples in its wake.

Shocked, she stared across the surface of the aqua water, disappointed that she would never see that bottle again.

Chapter Two

West Palm Beach, Florida

LISA'S FIRST DAY back at work started out like any other day. At 8 am sharp, she stepped off the elevator into the spacious lobby of the insurance agency where she worked. She'd started there in college part-time as a receptionist and had eventually worked her way up to a department supervisor.

"Hi, Millie." She approached the middle-aged receptionist sitting behind a circular oak desk. The words "Bahler & Bahler, Inc." hung in large gold letters on the wall behind the pudgy, dark-haired woman wearing a rose-colored business suit. "Did anything exciting happen in my absence?"

The Palm Beach and West Palm Beach branches were merging into one location. Construction of the new office building had been completed and the employees were expecting to receive the order to move in any day now.

Millie Katz adjusted her oversized reading glasses, trimmed with diamond-cut leaves and vines in Black Hills gold. "There's no word yet on the move-in date." Gold bangle bracelets tinkled on her arm as she pulled off her spectacles attached to a beaded chain around her neck. "Did you have a good time on your vacation?"

Lisa sighed. "I had a lovely week. Enchanted Island is so beautiful and it was really nice to finally meet all of the women in my book club."

She decided not to mention the part about stuffing the message in a bottle and tossing it out to sea. Millie would probably laugh at her and she didn't feel like explaining why they did it. Instead, she reached into her purse and pulled out a small Caribbean rum cake. "I brought you a little something to have with your coffee this morning."

Millie burst into a smile at the sight of the gold, hexagon-shaped box. "I've always wanted to try one of these. "Thank you, sweetie!"

"Enjoy!" Lisa waved goodbye and walked toward her office, greeting the women in her department one by one as she passed their cubicles. Once in her office, she flipped on the light and dropped her purse into a bottom drawer of her desk. Everything looked to be in the same order she'd left it except for the huge pile of correspondence and files overflowing the in-box on her credenza. She turned on her computer and winced at the number of new emails waiting for her, knowing it would take most of the morning to read and answer them all.

She wanted to catch up on her work today so

she could leave her office tonight without a long "To-Do" list for tomorrow sitting on her desk. Rob had asked her out to dinner and she didn't want work issues lingering in the back of her mind while they were discussing the "important" topic he'd mentioned in his last phone call. She glanced at her bare ring finger and smiled to herself, imagining his engagement ring on her hand.

Her thoughts turned to more immediate issues and she sighed, staring at the pile of paperwork sitting on her credenza. "I need some coffee before I tackle this mess." As she walked away, she heard something fall off her in-box and land on the floor with a loud splat, but she ignored it and headed toward the breakroom. It would still be there when she got back.

She found her desk phone ringing when she returned. The caller ID read M. Katz. "Yeah, Millie, what's up?"

"I don't know," Millie said in a voice so low Lisa could barely hear it, "but I'll bet it has something to do with the merger."

"What do you mean? What's wrong? Why are you whispering?" She caught herself whispering, too. Shaking her head, she set down her coffee cup.

"Two executives from the Palm Beach office just showed up and they're in the conference room right now, meeting with our executive director."

"Great!" Lisa retrieved the fallen file jacket and papers from the carpeted floor. "They're probably going over the schedule for the move."

"I don't think so. They brought along a team of counselors."

"What?" Lisa straightened. "Is the team from Duran and Associates?"

"Yes…"

Oh-oh. Duran and Associates provided free assistance to Bahler & Bahler employees for mental health, addiction and work/life issues. To have a team of their people on hand suggested something critical had happened and management was about to break the news to everyone.

"Thanks, Millie. Keep me posted."

She hung up, but her hand was still clutching the phone when it rang again. The caller ID showed C. Madison, the executive director's assistant. Her hand shook as she picked it up. "This is Lisa. How may I help you, Carrie?"

"Mr. Poole would like to see you right away." Carrie's usual cheerful voice sounded strained, as though she was under a great deal of pressure. "He's in the conference room."

Lisa's heart began to slam in her chest. "I—I'll be right there."

Why do they want to see me? What the heck

is going on?

She left her office, passed the reception area and walked around the corner to the conference room. Mr. Poole, the executive director, sat at the long, oval conference table with the two executives from the Palm Beach office. His chiseled face looked ashen. She walked in and shut the door behind her.

"Have a seat, Lisa," he said, sounding friendly, but nervous.

She pulled out a chair and sat down opposite the three men.

Mr. Poole cleared his throat. "The reason we've called you into this meeting is to inform you that this office is being closed. As of today, your employment is terminated."

Her jaw dropped. "Are you saying I'm fired?"

One of the executives, a dark-haired man, fortyish, wearing a black Brooks Brothers suit and red silk tie spoke up. "You're being laid off." He glanced at the open file in front of him. "Along with your last paycheck, you'll be compensated for the remainder of your unused vacation and given a week of severance pay for each year of service with the company."

"Yes, but—"

He looked up. "If you feel you need to speak with a counselor, we have a team on the premises to assist you. If not, you'll go straight to HR to conduct your exit interview and to sign the necessary paperwork. Then you'll clean out your office and leave." He gave her a cold smile. "Do you have any questions?"

She blinked, barely able to think much less speak. She'd worked for this company for ten years. How could they do this to her?

"You told us a year ago that no one would lose their jobs. You said the merger would simply combine the two offices."

You lied to us—to all of us. You allowed us to believe our jobs were safe so we'd all keep working until the end; until you didn't need us any longer...

"I'm not at liberty to address that issue. So," he said curtly and flipped the file closed, "I believe we're finished here. You're excused, Ms. Kaye. HR is expecting you."

Mr. Poole stood and extended his hand. "Thank you, Lisa, for all of your years of good service. You did a great job." His cold, clammy palm grasped hers. "If you need a reference for your next position, feel free to list my name on your application."

She stood, nearly overcome with empathy for him. She only had to go through this once. He had to repeat the same scenario with every one of his employees—all one hundred and fifty. "Thank you, Mr. Poole. You're more than kind." Then she walked out, so numb she could barely find her way to the Human Resources Department.

On the way back from her interview in HR, she passed the reception area. Millie sat covering her face with her hands, sobbing. After comforting Millie, she approached the women in her department, confirming the news that had already spread through the office faster than a speeding bullet. They were all losing their jobs...

A stack of foldable cartons leaned against the wall outside her office. Lisa dragged a couple inside her space and began to sift through ten years of memories of her career at Bahler & Bahler. She had finished packing the last box when her cell phone chirped. Fishing it out of her purse, she read on the screen that Rob had sent her a text. She wanted to talk to him directly, but he traveled extensively for his job as a pharmaceutical rep and often had last-minute meetings that kept him too busy to call.

Must cancel dinner tonight. Emergency meeting. Rob

She groaned with disappointment as she read his message. She'd looked forward to tonight. What else could go wrong today?

"Hey, Barb," she said as she walked out of her office and peered over the top of the closest cubicle. "Millie told me you're getting a group together to meet in the bar across the street for lunch. Count me in."

Lisa: Beach Brides Series

****

Later that afternoon, Lisa walked into her living room and collapsed on the sofa. What an exhausting day! The stress of the layoff had drained a lot of emotional energy from her. She'd spent the morning closing down her office, packing up her personal items and hauling everything out to her car. The wine at lunch had soothed her nerves, but now she didn't have enough energy to haul her boxes into the house.

Her cell phone rang. Hoping Rob had found time to call, she scrambled to dig it out of her purse. Instead, the caller turned out to be a good friend.

"Hi, Terri," she said slowly as she stretched out on her powder blue sofa and slung one arm over her eyes.

"What's the matter, Lisa? You sound depressed." Terri Barna's usual perky voice sounded apprehensive. Elevator music and a cacophony of voices echoed in the background of the department store where Terri worked as a general manager.

"It's Monday and I have a headache," Lisa replied with a loud yawn, purposely avoiding the subject of her current employment situation. "I mean, it's tough to get back into the usual routine after a great vacation." *Especially after you've been given a pink slip and drowned your sorrows in wine.* "Are you calling me from work?"

"Hold on a second," Terri said and covered the receiver with her hand as she spoke to someone. "Okay, I'm back. Sorry for the interruption. Yes, I'm working, but I've got tonight off and I don't want to spend it watching television. If you're not busy, would you like to meet me for dinner and a movie? There's a romantic comedy called *Falling in Love in L.A.* playing at the Rialto. We could catch the early show and have spaghetti afterward at that quaint little restaurant across the street."

Lisa groaned silently, her arm still draped over her eyes. She didn't feel like going anywhere, but she did want to see that movie. It had received great reviews.

Maybe I should hang out with Terri tonight. This hasn't been the best of days and I could use some cheering up...

"Okay," she said with a sigh, "I could use some company today. Do you want to meet in front of the theater?"

"Sure," Terri replied. "I can be there by five-thirty. Bring your umbrella. It's supposed to rain."

"See you then. Bye."

Lisa had just enough time to freshen up and drive across town to the theater.

Terri waited in front of the box office under a hot pink umbrella, wearing violet leggings and a matching hip-length tunic. "I can smell the aroma of freshly popped corn all the way out here," she said as Lisa hurried toward her. "Come on—let's buy our tickets so we can get some before the movie starts."

After the movie, they dashed across the street to Botticelli's Italian Restaurant for pasta and garlic toast. The small, family-owned establishment hadn't changed in years, but its old-world charm and southern Italian red sauce dishes had withstood the test of time. Lisa and Terri walked into a crowded, softly lit dining room decorated with hand-painted murals, white linen tablecloths and a polished mahogany bar. Classic Italian folk music and the pungent aroma of spicy sausage saturated the air.

As they waited for the host to seat them, Lisa casually glanced around the room. At first, she blinked, not quite believing what she saw. Once she realized her eyes weren't deceiving her, her emotions went into a tailspin.

Tucked in a corner on the other side of the room, Rob relaxed at a table for two. Though he had his back to Lisa, she recognized his dark, curly hair brushing the collar of his pine green sport jacket. She'd seen that jacket on him many times and knew it well—she'd given it to him on his birthday. When he turned his head, she saw his profile and her heart fell to her feet.

He sat facing a beautiful blonde in a black sequined dress with sparkling jewelry. Lisa stared in shock as the woman gazed into his eyes, her outstretched hands on the table intertwined with his. The way she communicated to Rob without words indicated she shared more than friendship with him. She knew him intimately.

He lied to me. He called off our evening to spend it with another woman...

Suddenly, everything he'd ever said to her came into question—every time he'd had to cancel at the last minute, every weekend he supposedly had to work...

"What's the matter, Lisa?" Terri frowned. "What are you gawking at?"

"Look at the couple in the corner, next to the mural of Venice."

Terri went silent at first then gasped as she took in the scene. "Isn't that Rob? Who is that woman with him?"

Lisa stared helplessly, her mind numbed for the second time today. "I've never seen her before, but I think I know."

Rob and his companion suddenly rose from the table. As they made their way through the crowded room toward the exit, their server followed close on their heels. "Thank you and have a nice evening, Mr. and Mrs. Mancuso." The young man held up the check presenter, indicating his gratitude for a generous gratuity. "Congratulations!"

Lisa and Terri both heard the server and stared at each other in surprise. Though he didn't elaborate on what the couple had come for dinner to celebrate, Lisa instinctively understood what the server meant. She knew now why Rob wanted to meet with her and what he had planned to say.

He didn't deserve to get away with this. She wanted to confront him in front of his wife, but she knew it would probably do more harm than good. Instead of staging a nasty scene, she darted into the ladies' room to avoid him.

Terri burst into the small room after her and grabbed her by the arms. "What are you doing hiding in here? Get out there and give that cheating dog a piece of your mind!"

Lisa pushed the door shut and fell against it, tears spilling from her eyes. "What's the point? He's married to her. Didn't you hear the server call them Mr. and Mrs. Mancuso? That rock on her hand looked bigger than the Hope diamond. I couldn't help noticing the pallor in her face and the dark circles under her eyes. She's pregnant."

Terri stared at her incredulously. "You take one look at her and conclude all of that?"

"It's obvious!"

Terri's jaw clenched. "You're not going to let him get away with this, are you?"

"What good would it do to seek revenge? Even

Denise Devine

if I wanted to confront him, don't you realize it's my word against his? If I caused a scene in front of his wife, he would simply deny it and call me a liar—or worse—to discredit me and make me look like a fool." Lisa balled her fists. "I refuse to lower myself to his level."

"His wife needs to know the truth!"

"She wouldn't believe me." Lisa reached into her purse and pulled out a tissue. "Besides, do you really think that would stop Rob from cheating on her again? I doubt it." She sniffled and dabbed at her nose. "The fact that she's married to a lying, two-timing rat is not my problem." Her eyes filled with fresh, angry tears. "*He* isn't my problem any longer, either. I don't want anything to do with him ever again."

Terri opened the door slightly and peered through the crack. "They're at the door. He's helping her with her shawl."

Lisa peeked through the tiny crack and watched Rob spread the shawl across the woman's narrow shoulders. Her heart ached as though it would break in two as Rob gazed lovingly into his wife's eyes then dipped his head and kissed her gently on the lips.

How could she have been so blind when the telltale signs had been there all along?

We only see what we want to see...

Lisa: Beach Brides Series

"They're leaving. Come on, let's go." Terri swung the door open wide and grabbed Lisa by the arm. "Never mind dinner, we're going to the bar."

They walked through the misty rain to a small piano lounge two blocks away and sat on a sofa by the crackling fireplace drinking glasses of Chianti. Lisa opened up to Terri about losing her job.

"Gosh, one week you're having the time of your life on vacation and the next week your life turns totally upside down." Terri held up her glass to signal to the cocktail server for another round. "What are you going to do?"

"Something I would never have considered a week ago." Lisa stared at the orange flames in the small, but cozy fireplace. "I'm going to put my townhouse up for sale and move to Enchanted Island to manage my Aunt Elsie's bed and breakfast hotel."

I need a new adventure, she thought, anxious to return to the most memorable place of her childhood. She remembered the crazy message she'd stuffed in the antique bottle and tossed into the bay three days ago. It didn't seem so unrealistic anymore. She'd always wanted to be that carefree, audacious girl, but the demands of life had constantly gotten in the way. What would it be like to live year-round on a beautiful Caribbean island? She didn't have a clue, but she was about to find out.

Chapter Three

Miami, Florida

Fifteen Months Later - The Month of October

SHAWN WELLS WALKED into the lobby of the Hibiscus Hotel at 8 am, bracing himself for a meeting with his father. His assistant had called him on his way to work and given him the bad news. Wyndom Wells, CEO of the Wells Hotel Corporation had arrived earlier than expected and already had the staff in an uproar with his unrealistic demands and imperious manner. Wyn lived in New York City and only paid Shawn a visit when he had something to say that he didn't want to handle over the phone. Shawn wondered what had happened to get his father worked up this time.

The elderly doorman wearing a black suit and top hat greeted Shawn with a smile. "Good morning, Mr. Wells. How was your vacation?"

"Terrific, James," Shawn replied with a nod. "I've uploaded my pictures and videos to Facebook and Instagram. Check them out when you get time."

"I will surely do that, Mr. Wells. You have a

wonderful day now."

"Thank you, James." *Things will definitely improve as soon as I find out what my father has up his sleeve.* "You have a great day, too."

He passed through the double set of entrance doors into the two-story marble and glass lobby, tensing from the stress steadily building within him. His assistant, Lucia Perez, stood waiting for him with her trusty clipboard in hand; her oversized black-rimmed glasses were perched on the end of her nose as she studied Shawn's itinerary for the day.

"Good morning, Shawn, and welcome back," she said with a Cuban accent. Her navy suit, flat shoes and black hair twisted into a bun at the nape of her neck mirrored the serious attitude she maintained on the job. "You have a busy schedule today." She flipped through the pages attached to her clipboard, scribbling notes as they walked to the elevators. "I set the meeting with your father for nine o'clock to give you some time to clean up your desk and skim over your emails." She let out a frustrated huff. "But, as I told you on the phone, he showed up twenty minutes ago and is having a fit because you're not here yet. I've ordered the chef to send coffee, rolls and fruit to your office *immediately*."

She checked her clipboard again. "You have a two-hour staff meeting with your managers at ten—" She looked up from her schedule, tapping her chin with her pen. "That's assuming your father is finished with you by then. If not, I'll have to adjust everything accordingly." They reached the elevator bank. The doors to the closest elevator opened and Shawn held the door for Lucia to enter first. "Oh, and I made a reservation for noon at Vanelli's for your luncheon with Brittany..."

The rest of Lucia's words faded into a blur as Shawn stepped into the elevator and focused his thoughts on his fiancée, Brittany Stone. Brittany had thrown a tantrum of biblical proportions when she found out he'd signed up for another dig on the outskirts of Jerusalem. She hated getting her hands dirty. For that matter, she hated anything that involved dirt *and* sweating, so asking her to accompany him on a volunteer gig had been definitely out of the question. Brittany's vision of the ideal vacation involved a fruity cocktail under an umbrella on a tropical beach somewhere and she couldn't understand why he pursued such a gritty hobby at a time when he should be relaxing. She'd refused to go—as usual—and had accused him of giving it more priority than her.

He stepped off the elevator on the second floor, parting company with Lucia and walked the short distance to his office suite, wondering what Wyn wanted this time. Hopefully, his father had good news about the construction of their newest hotel on the strip in Las Vegas.

Wyn sat behind Shawn's desk, riffling through his papers, looking thinner, strained and definitely grayer than the last time Shawn saw him. Since the death of Shawn's mother, Wyn's health had been steadily declining. His testy disposition hadn't changed, though.

"Looking for something, Dad?"

Wyn glanced up, his ice blue eyes appraising Shawn's appearance. "You're tanned. You must have spent a lot of time sightseeing in Greece."

Shawn stopped in front of his desk and stared at the mess Wyn had made of his files. "I went to Israel on an archaeological dig."

Wyn shrugged, his bored expression suggesting Shawn's archaeological escapades were of minor importance. It irritated Shawn to no end how little attention his father gave to anything that didn't involve the family business. "Are you ready to get back to work?"

"What are you saying?" Shawn perked up. Construction on the Desert Indigo Casino and Hotel in Las Vegas was nearing completion when he left on vacation. "Are the decorators getting ready to start on the interior of the Indigo? I need to fly out there and begin planning the grand opening!"

Wyn shoved a couple papers back into its folder. "The target date for the soft opening is a month from today. Your brother has been in Las Vegas for several weeks, supervising the decorating and working with our PR agency to organize the grand opening."

"What?" He couldn't believe it. Wyn had purposely left him out of the final stage. "Why is Ian opening the Desert Indigo? You told me that was *my* hotel. *I'm* the one who is supposed to manage it!"

Wyn stood up, his square jaw set. "I'm moving to Nevada. My offices will be in the Desert Indigo until I retire. Then Ian will take over everything."

Shawn gripped the edge of his desk to keep himself steady. "Ian is taking over the corporation? When did you decide this?" *When did you two go behind my back and cut me out?*

"I spoke with him yesterday," Wyn stated. "Ian has worked closely with me for years and I've decided he's ready to take over my position." He tossed the folder on the desk. "You still have a lot to learn, son. When the time comes, you'll get a share of the business, but Ian will always have principal control."

Wyn's words struck like an arrow through Shawn's heart. Wyn had always led him to believe that he and his older brother would share the corporation equally. Suddenly, everything had changed. Why?

"I cleaned up the Hibiscus and turned it around, just like you wanted. I raised the occupancy rates, improved the hotel's rating, found ways to reduce staff and made a significant increase in the bottom line." The volume of his voice rose as his anger grew. He knew everyone on the administration floor could hear him, but he didn't care. "I *always* do what you ask and I do it well. I've proven I'm qualified to share the responsibility of running this corporation!"

"Yes, you've done a great job making this hotel turn a profit and I'm proud of what you've accomplished here." Wyn walked around the desk and placed his palms on Shawn's shoulders. "This is what you do best, son. You're smart and efficient. When you take on a challenge, you keep at it until you've mastered it. You wouldn't be happy doing Ian's job."

"I'll decide what makes me happy and what doesn't!" Shawn glared at his father. "So, what's next for me? Where do I go from here? Are you reassigning me to Vegas to clean Ian's office every night?"

Wyn dropped his hands. "Actually, I've got an interesting job for you," he said, ignoring Shawn's caustic remarks. "I need your expert development skills to accomplish a project on a land deal I'm putting together."

Irritated at Wyn for not discussing it with him first, Shawn straightened and placed his hands on his hips. "Land deals are for our lawyers. I don't know the first thing about the legalities of real estate."

Wyn casually eased himself onto the edge of

Shawn's desk, but the pallor of his skin and his shallow, rapid breathing indicated he needed to get off his feet. "I've signed a purchase agreement on Enchanted Island for six acres of land abutting the Amaryllis to build a retail complex. The request for proposals has already been published."

"Are you kidding me?" Shawn responded with a harsh laugh, his disappointment showing through loud and clear. "The Amaryllis has only fifty rooms! It's the smallest hotel we own on a postage stamp of an island fifty miles off the coast of Florida. Why don't you hire a general contractor to take care of it?"

Win's face flushed with anger. He always bristled when Shawn had the audacity to challenge him. "You and Pete LaMaur have been reassigned to Enchanted Island to close on the land and manage the construction project. Your assistant general manager will take over here. You leave next week."

"Wait a minute, Dad." Shawn held up one hand to halt the discussion. "I haven't agreed to this yet. I need to talk to Brittany about it first—"

"Don't argue with me. This is why Ian got a promotion and you didn't." Wyn slid off the desk. "I'm still in charge and when I give one of my sons an order, I expect it to be carried out." He turned and walked toward the door. "I want that project completed in time for the busy season. Is that understood? When you finish the job, we'll continue our discussion on your partnership in the corporation."

Wyn walked out, leaving Shawn to stare after him, questioning the wisdom of even bothering to pursue a partnership in the corporation.

****

"Look, Brittany, it's only going to be for a few months." Shawn pushed his plate of blackened grouper aside. The fish was delicious, but Brittany's disappointing response had made him lose interest in his lunch. "The project has to be completed in time for when the snowbirds come."

Brittany's golden brows arched over her deep blue eyes. "The what..."

"You know—retirees from the northern states. After Christmas, they flock to warmer climate to get away from the cold and the snow. They're the baby boomer generation and they have a lot of money to spend. Dad wants the shops open by the time the busy season starts."

"Dad wants this, Dad wants that." She rolled her eyes. "You're thirty-five years old, Shawn. It's time you stood up to your father and demanded that he stop treating you like a common laborer. You're his *son* and you deserve an executive position in the corporation."

Brittany's parents always gave her anything she wanted. She couldn't understand why his father didn't operate the same way.

Shawn let out an exasperated sigh. "Ian and I know better than to demand anything from Wyn. He's the boss and the boss always gets the last word." *Dad has always been that way and he isn't going to change, no matter what I say.*

The server appeared. "Are you finished with your lunch, sir?" Shawn nodded without looking up.

"I don't have a choice, Brit. I have to complete that project on Enchanted Island. Will you come with me?"

She picked up her phone. "And do what? Walk along the beach and collect seashells while you're working twelve to sixteen hours a day?" Her eyes narrowed. "No."

"Why not? You love the Caribbean and this particular island isn't just a beautiful place, it's naturally heart-shaped, too. We'd have the ultimate vacation on a romantic locale that would last for months."

"Exactly," she snapped and dropped her phone into her purse. "I'll be stuck on a remote island shaped like a valentine with nothing to do *for months*. I won't be able to hang out with my friends, go shopping at the mall or have dinner with my family. What about my modeling career? I need to keep in touch with my agent and the stupid place probably doesn't even have the Internet yet. Or a decent coffee shop."

He laughed. "Yes, it has all of that. You can fly or take a water taxi to the mainland any time you want. It's only fifty miles away." He reached across the table and took her hand. "Look, we'll have all that time to be together in a fairytale setting. Just you and me. Please, Brittany, come with me."

She whisked her long golden hair into a jeweled clip. "I won't be happy if I go and I don't believe you'll enjoy being stranded there for months, either. I'm asking you—for once in your life—stand up to your father. Tell him to send someone else. He's not going to fire you. He'll give you whatever you want."

"You know I can't do that, Brit. It's more than a job. It's family; it's the only thing I know."

"You're choosing your job over me?" She jerked her hand away. "That's unacceptable. If you're not going to put me first, there's no reason for me to waste any more time on this relationship." She shoved back her chair and stood. "The engagement is off. I refuse to settle for second place. If you won't make me a priority in your life, I'll find someone who will. And don't bother to call me later, expecting me to change my mind because I won't! I'm blocking your number."

She pulled off her engagement ring, tossed it into her glass of iced tea and stormed out.

****

Denise Devine

Enchanted Island, East Caribbean

Nine Days Later

Shawn wandered through the gift shop at the Amaryllis Boutique Hotel, checking out the space. This merchant would likely move to the retail complex and once she had vacated the room he planned to turn it into a coffee shop. She sold an eclectic collection of artwork, unusual and one-of-a-kind articles.

As he browsed a display on the back wall, one item caught his eye, a blue antique bottle sealed with a synthetic stopper. He reached up and pulled it off the glass shelf to examine it.

"It's an interesting little gem, isn't it?"

He turned around to find the shopkeeper standing behind him, a heavy woman wearing a purple flowered caftan. She had thick, flaming red hair, heavy gold earrings and sparkling gemstone rings on all her fingers.

"I like antiques," he said. "Do you have more?"

"No, but there's a shop in Morganville that does," she said in a British accent. "A local chap sold this one to me last year. He found it floating in a small pool of water between a couple large rocks down by the point. It must have come ashore with the tide. I didn't have any idea what to charge for it so I set it in the cupboard temporarily and then forgot about it. This morning I was cleaning out the shelves and found it collecting dust behind a box of Christmas lights." She tapped a long red fingernail against the bottle. "Look, there's a message in it."

Shawn held it up to the light. "That's amazing. I wonder how long it had been bobbing around in the ocean." Judging by the synthetic cork, it hadn't been there long. Still, it intrigued him. He shook the bottle to see if it held anything else, but could only make out the narrowly folded message. Filled with sand, it would make an interesting paperweight for his desk. He handed the bottle to her and reached into his pocket for his wallet. "I'll take it."

She rang up the sale, wrapped it in tissue paper and placed it in a shiny red plastic bag. "Here you go, Mr. Wells."

He remembered her name from their introduction yesterday when he'd personally met with every hotel employee. "Just call me Shawn, okay Mavis?"

She grinned. "Shawn, it 'tis then."

Shawn left the shop and walked into the hotel lobby. The sound of chanting drew his attention to a group of women carrying signs in front of the building. At the same time, Pete LaMaur bolted across the stone plaza and burst through the front doors.

"What's going on, LaMaur?"

As the doors closed behind Pete, the warm, Caribbean breeze rushing through the opening ruffled his blue square-bottomed shirt. He ran his hand over his short brown hair. "It's an organized protest. Some group from Morganville is objecting to our plan to build the shops. They say it's going to ruin the island's economy."

Shawn stared at the motley assortment of brightly dressed women parading back and forth with their homemade signs. "We've only been here two days and people are already objecting to the development? News travels fast around here."

Pete answered with a nervous laugh. "That's for sure. Two days is light speed when you're talking *island time.*"

One of the first things they learned upon arriving on the island was the difference between American time and island time. Going by American time meant simply being on time. Going by island time meant the person would "get there when he got there." *No problem, mon.*

"It must be a pretty sensitive issue to cause such quick opposition." Pete stared through the glass doors at the women and scratched his head, his brows knitting together. "How do you want to handle it?"

"There's only one thing we can do. We'll have to go out there and talk to them."

Lisa: Beach Brides Series

Pete's jaw dropped. "Are you crazy? Talk to a bunch of protesting women? They'll tear us to pieces!"

Shawn began to walk toward the front entrance. "I guess that's the chance we'll have to take. We certainly can't ignore them." He strolled across the plaza to greet the protesters congregating on the sidewalk.

That's when he saw her...

Slender and petite with elbow-length dark hair, she stood apart from the group wearing sandals and a short yellow dress. A jade teardrop pendant hanging from a gold chain adorned her long, graceful neck. It matched her eyes. For a moment, he stood mesmerized, unable to pull his gaze from her until Pete appeared at his side and murmured, "Good luck, pal. You're gonna need it."

Shawn cleared his throat and refocused his attention on the matter at hand. "Good afternoon, ladies. I'm Shawn Wells, the general manager of the Amaryllis Hotel and this is Peter LaMaur, the manager of maintenance. What can we do for you?"

A tall, Bahamian woman stepped forward wearing a long lavender sundress with rows of silver beads sewn along the round, low-cut neckline. Her thick, spiraled curls of ebony hair lifted in the breeze, bouncing playfully about her neck and shoulders. "You can stop this development before it ruins our island," she said with a throaty, Caribbean accent.

The words ending with an *r* sound were pronounced *ah*.

The women cheered and raised their signs.

"Take your fancy ideas and go back to where you came from," the woman continued. "Just because we are a territory of the US, that doesn't mean we want to be Americanized. Enchanted Island is a beautiful place with its own identity and we intend to keep it that way."

"You're right." Shawn put forth his friendliest smile. "The island is a wonderful place and the last thing we want to do is spoil its natural beauty."

"Then tear up your purchase agreement and leave!"

The women began to all talk at once.

"Girls! Girls!" Pete raised his hands to call the crowd to attention. "There's no need to—"

"Who are you calling *gyal*," the Bahamian woman shot back in a challenging tone as she confronted Pete nose-to-nose. "We are business*women* and we demand respect. You got a problem with that?"

Pete stood motionless, locked into her wide, distinctive eyes, the color of espresso coffee. "No..."

"Then I will accept your apology." She jammed her hands on her slim hips, her golden arms jingling with a stack of metal bracelets on each one.

He swallowed hard, as though he had a difficult time concentrating. "I...we...w-what did you say?"

"What—you got a hearing problem, too?"

The woman in the yellow dress moved to her side and whispered something into her ear. They both turned toward Shawn.

"Let's start over," the woman said in a serious, but feminine voice. "I'm Lisa Kaye, the spokesperson for the Island Women's Business League and this is the group's president," she gestured toward her beautiful, but angry companion, "Shakara Allain."

Lisa turned briefly toward the crowd with a sweeping motion of her hand. "Everyone here owns some type of retail establishment in the Morganville business district. We're opposed to the development proposal your corporation has submitted for approval. We believe it's detrimental to the island's economy and a direct assault on the environment. Since the council won't listen to us, we've organized this rally to voice our objections to you."

Her thorough knowledge of his proposal took him by surprise. "I understand your concern," Shawn replied, seeing the need to divert the public demonstration into a closed-door session. "Why don't you ladies step inside and have refreshments while we discuss the issue?"

The women stared at each other as though

suspicious of his openness and willingness to cooperate. He gestured toward the lobby. "Please, be my guests. Right this way."

The group deposited their signs in a neat stack next to a wide planter and gingerly walked into the hotel.

Pete stood transfixed on Shakara Allain as she followed the group into the building, her tall, slender figure moving with the grace of a ballerina.

"What a goddess," he murmured. "I think I'm in love..."

Shawn tried unsuccessfully to suppress a grin as he patted Pete on the shoulder. "You'll get over it. Come on, it looks like we need to do some major damage control."

They ushered the women into a sunny lobby of marble floors, white woodwork and tall arched windows shaded by mature palm trees surrounding the building. Pete led them past the reception area arranged with aqua damask furniture, fresh flowers and local artwork to the open stairway that took them up to a mezzanine and Shawn's office suite.

"Susan," Shawn said to the blonde woman standing behind the registration counter, "call the kitchen and have the staff bring Switchta and cookies for a dozen people up to my office immediately." He grabbed a bowl of fresh fruit off the counter and bounded up the stairs, opening the double doors to his office.

"Come in, ladies, and have a seat."

Shawn deposited the bag with his antique bottle on the credenza behind his desk and placed the fruit bowl in the center of his conference table. It only seated six people, so the rest had to stand while Pete set up additional chairs.

"Refreshments are on the way," Shawn announced as he faced the group. "In the meantime, let's start the discussion. I'd like to hear your objections to the development."

Lisa Kaye stepped forward and folded her arms, her body language indicating she expected a confrontation. Close up, her dark hair looked like strands of silk against her sunny yellow chemise. He found her intriguing and wondered what type of business she owned. "We've obtained a copy of the report you submitted to the council last week to buy the Regis property," she said in a business-like tone, "and to build on it what basically amounts to a strip mall."

"We refer to it as 'The Shops at Enchanted Isle'."

Her direct, cynical stare never wavered. "And just what makes these shops more *enchanting* than the historic district in Morganville?"

"They will be upscale, one-of-a-kind stores."

"That's not what your report says." She pulled a thick sheaf of papers from her leather shoulder bag and held up a page that she'd marked with a green highlighter. "On page seven there is a list of the types of businesses that will fill the mall and it's almost an exact duplicate of the most popular shops in Morganville. For instance, the first business on your list is handcrafted jewelry. That's Shakara's shop. Another one is a gift boutique that sells needlework crafted exclusively by the women on this island. That's my Aunt Elsie's shop. The list goes on and on. This is not merely a coincidence. You've definitely done your homework." She looked up, focusing on him with an accusing glare. "It appears, Mr. Wells, that you are targeting our businesses to pull the tourist trade away from us and literally bankrupt the downtown retail district so you can have one hundred percent of the market share for your own shops."

Shawn floundered with confusion at the specific reference to the report.

That wasn't in the final draft I read before Dad emailed it to the council secretary.

Sweat began to form on the back of his neck. He looked like a fool not knowing what facts his own proposal contained. Wyn must have made some last-minute edits, but neglected to tell him about them. Wyn's failure to communicate the changes angered him, but he pushed the issue out of his mind for now.

"Ms. Kaye," he said boldly, "I'm the project

manager and I will make the final decision on who leases the spaces when they're ready for occupancy. I assure you, I'll make certain my shops don't directly compete with yours, as that wouldn't be in the best interests of anyone. You have my word on it."

He turned to his desk and pulled out the file with a freshly printed copy of the report, intending to study it thoroughly after the meeting to make sure Wyn hadn't changed anything else.

A server from the kitchen knocked on the door and entered, rolling in a stainless-steel cart with pitchers of chilled Switchta, the Bahamian version of lemonade, and a platter of coconut-mango cookies. Everyone took a break, indulging in cookies and friendly chatter.

Shawn stood next to Lisa, still holding the folder containing the proposal. He understood the reason for her cool attitude toward him, but it put him at a disadvantage. "You don't approve of me, do you?"

She gave him a sideways glance. "No, and to be perfectly honest, I don't trust you, either."

Her directness didn't surprise him, but the double accusation did. "You get right to the point, don't you?"

The server offered her a cookie. She raised her left palm and declined. She wore no rings on either hand. "At least I mean what I say."

"And you think I don't?"

She gestured toward the manila folder in his hand. As she moved, the sweet, floral scent of her perfume filled his nostrils, distracting him. Their gazes met and as he stared into her wide jade eyes, he found it impossible to pull away.

Stick to business, he chided himself. *The last thing you need is to become attracted to a woman on this island and get tangled up in a relationship. You're not going to be here long so don't complicate things by starting something you don't intend to finish.*

"Everything you say is the opposite of what you have in writing," Lisa retorted. "What guarantee do we have that you'll follow through with the promises you've given lip service to today?"

"I gave you my word that my shops won't directly compete with yours. What else can I do?"

She prefaced her reply with an impatient sigh. "Mr. Wells—"

"Everyone just calls me Shawn."

"All I'm saying, *Shawn*, is that our group is composed of average citizens trying to make a decent living. You're representing a corporation with money and a team of lawyers to fight your battles for you. We're no match for your resources or apparent influence with the council, but we're committed to fighting this all the way if you change your mind and go with what's in the report."

"Then meet me for lunch tomorrow and we'll go over the plans together." The words came out of his mouth before he realized what he'd said. Now that he'd spoken, he couldn't take them back. "I-I just want you to be informed of all the facts so you can report back to your association."

She started to object, her plump, rose-colored lips parting slightly, but then she paused. "All right," she said slowly, as though weighing her options. "What time?"

"I'll meet you at noon in the Bayside Café."

The hotel's open-air café was the island's most popular venue with its seaside view of Azure Bay and the pink sand beach. He'd have to rearrange his schedule to make it on time, but he didn't mind. He needed to form a relationship with the island business community and this was a good place to start. Or did this just happen to be a convenient excuse to get to know *her* better?

Their gazes held again. "I'm looking forward to it," Lisa said, though the skeptical look in her eyes indicated otherwise.

Her phone chirped, interrupting them. "Excuse me." She pulled out her phone and checked the screen. "I'm needed at the shop. I have to go."

She turned to the group. "Ladies, I've arranged to meet with Shawn tomorrow to review his drawings for the mall and discuss the specifics so that I can report the information back to you. Is that acceptable to everyone?"

The women briefly talked among themselves and unanimously agreed.

She bid goodbye to everyone and left.

The women began to file out behind her, a few at a time. Shawn sat at his desk and flipped open the folder. He'd begun to study the revised proposal when he looked up and saw Pete holding the door for Shakara.

She sashayed to the doorway and stopped. "So, you're an engineer? You know how to fix things, Pee-tah?"

"You name it," Pete said, puffing out his chest. "I can build it or fix it."

"H-m-m-m..." Shakara tapped her cheek with one finger tipped with an inch-long nail painted in sparkly maroon. "Are you for hire? What do you charge?"

Pete burst into a boyish grin. "Whatever you need, I'd be happy to lend a hand. My price is an ice-cold beer."

She placed her finger under his chin. "You're kind of cute, bey," she cooed, her voice velvety smooth. She leaned closer. "Come to my shop. I'll show you my *plumbing*."

Pete swallowed hard, his smile widening with fascination. "Any time..."

"I'll give you a call." She waved goodbye and walked out.

Pete leaned in the doorway and stared after her like a rock star groupie.

"Earth to Pete," Shawn said, grinning at his friend.

"Huh?" Pete turned around.

Shawn could almost see stars twinkling in his eyes. "It didn't take her long to get you wrapped around her finger."

"Hey, what did you get at the gift shop," Pete asked as he approached the desk, obviously trying to divert the discussion away from his attraction to Shakara Allain.

Shawn snatched the red bag off his credenza and pulled out the wad of tissue paper protecting his purchase. He tore away the paper. "Look," he said and held up the blue bottle to the light to show Pete the folded note. "It's a message in a bottle."

Pete squinted to check it out. "That's cool. Are you going to open it?" He laughed. "It's probably the message from someone's fortune cookie."

Curious, Shawn pulled out the cork and shook the message onto his desk. He unfolded it and stared at the faded, handwritten words on the page. "It's a poem." As he scanned the lines he began to chuckle. Whoever wrote this had a cute sense of humor.

To Whom it may concern,

I'm an adventurous girl, who'd love to see the world, but I don't have the money or the time.

If I met someone, though, who liked to travel for fun, he'd become a best friend of mine.

I love the mountains, the seas, the rocks and the trees, and the Cairo Museum of Antiquities.

I've never seen a polar bear, or visited The World's Fair, or climbed the Eiffel Tower in France.

I want to see pyramids, ride a tram atop a rainforest, and visit Spain to watch the Flamenco dance.

Do you like piña coladas and strolling in the rain? Is there a special place in the world you'd love to see again?

If you're a guy who loves to fly, or cruise on the mighty sea, then give me a shout, tell me what you're all about, 'cause you might be the one for me.

IslandGirl#1@...

He saw her email at the bottom of the page and opened up his laptop. "So, she likes to travel," he murmured as he read through it a second time. "She listed her email address. I think I'll write back."

Chapter Four

LISA STARED AT the unopened email on her computer, surprised that after all this time someone had finally found the bottle and answered her message. She'd begun to think the bottle had been lost at sea.

She tapped her finger on the keyboard, undecided about whether or not she should open it. What if a crazy person, a man who stalked women online, had sent her the email? The men who tried to friend her on Facebook came to mind, the buff ones wearing military uniforms. The women in her Romantic Hearts Book Club online referred to them as trolls. With any luck, the man would be living on the other side of the world, but she had no way of knowing whether he lived fifteen minutes away or fifteen thousand miles away. The possibility of someone actually traveling to this island to stalk her gave her the creeps. She shivered at the thought.

The email address gave no indication whether the sender was a woman or a man, but the blank subject line didn't strike her as a woman's way of replying to her message.

"You'd better get moving if you're going out

for lunch. Those rooms don't clean themselves!" Aunt Elsie's stern voice echoed from the kitchen.

Putting it off for now, Lisa exited out of the email account and closed the cover on her laptop. She had breakfast dishes to load into the dishwasher, rooms to clean and laundry to catch up on before meeting Shawn Wells for lunch. Aunt Elsie still handled most of the cooking for the six-bedroom bed and breakfast and managed her small gift shop on the premises, but she'd delegated all of the cleaning, maintenance and laundry to Lisa.

She jumped up from the desk in the small alcove they had set up for Internet access. "I'll be right there, Auntie," she said, using the island version for "aunt." Elsie didn't purposely mean to sound gruff, but after years of raising four rambunctious children, she'd never outgrown her "strict mother" mode. Widowed at thirty, Elsie had been forced to be mother, father and provider to her family. Above all, she had a heart of gold, and Lisa considered Elsie her second mom.

Lisa spent the morning doing chores and getting ready for her luncheon with Shawn. She chose a peach linen suit and a floral blouse with short sleeves and a jewel neckline.

Shortly after eleven, she booted up her laptop again, hoping to skim the message before leaving for the Amaryllis. She nervously opened the email account.

"Well, here I go." Before she could change her mind, she clicked on it, opened it up and read the email.

To Island Girl:

Your message I have read, and "Wow!" is what I said.

One thing I need to know, did you mean what you wrote? If so...

You could be the one for me, but tell me the truth—are you married or are you free?

I'll keep the bottle if you don't mind, it's the only one I have of its kind.

Every time I see the antique in blue, it'll remind me of Island Girl—of you.

City Boy

She couldn't stop laughing. Whoever wrote that email took the time to compose the poem with the same silly style to match her prose. He had not only a charming sense of humor, but an honest way with words as well. And he knew the bottle was an antique, definitely a point in his favor.

She didn't have time to compose a response, but she planned to make it a priority to send him a reply as soon as she got back from lunch.

Lunch! Oh, my gosh. I'm going to be late!

"I'm leaving, Auntie. I'll be back by three

o'clock for check-in." Since Elsie had the gift shop to run, Lisa needed to be there in case their guests had any special requests or asked for assistance with their bags.

Elsie stood in the kitchen doorway, wiping her hands on her flowered apron. The short, stout woman frowned with concern. "I've got a bad feeling about this new development at the Amaryllis Hotel. If it's a success, it's going to pull a lot of our business away and force us to close the gift shop."

"Don't worry, Auntie. I'll find out everything I can about the new shops and whether Shawn plans to expand the hotel, too. We'll find a way to keep our business going."

Elsie's white hair glistened in a knot on the crown of her head. She shoved a stray tuft behind one ear. "I hope so. *Somebody* has to do something about this. The resorts have taken away so much of our business already, I don't know if we can withstand much more."

Lisa tucked a long silk scarf in her purse and briskly walked two blocks under shady trees to the waterfront to catch a ride on a water taxi. She wore flat sandals for better footing on the uneven pavement. The last thing she needed was to trip and sprain her ankle or skin her knees.

At the waterfront, she descended the stone steps leading down to the dock and sprinted toward the covered taxi stand to catch the next water taxi

Lisa: Beach Brides Series

leaving the Morganville port at eleven-thirty. The small, canopied boat circled the island all day, dropping off passengers and picking up others at the Amaryllis hotel and the resorts, eventually making its way back to the main port in Morganville.

Lisa paid the driver and stepped into the boat. She put on her sunglasses then secured the scarf on her head and around her neck to keep her long hair from whipping in the wind.

Fifteen minutes later, she arrived at the Amaryllis with time to freshen up before meeting with Shawn.

Why am I making such a fuss over my appearance, she thought as she pulled off her scarf and walked toward the ladies' room to touch up her makeup and brush her hair. *This is a casual business meeting, not a date.* Somehow, though, it felt more like a first date than a professional appointment with another merchant.

The Bayside Café provided a wide view of Azure Bay. A railing enclosed with white lattice served as a partition between the guests and the outer courtyard of tropical plants that buffered them from the incredible pink sand beach along the water's edge.

As she walked toward the waiting area, she saw a tall, broad-shouldered man with dark hair conversing with another man. It was Shawn, looking relaxed in khaki pants and a light green linen shirt.

Denise Devine

The moment he saw her, he shook hands with the man and excused himself then briskly walked toward her. His warm smile and the way he focused on her—as though they were the only two people in the busy restaurant—sent butterflies fluttering through her stomach.

"Hello," he said, his hazel eyes softening. "I hope you brought your appetite because I've taken the liberty of setting up a special dish for your lunch."

"That sounds wonderful," Lisa said, wondering what prompted him to go to all that trouble. Did he have disappointing news and planned to get her in a good mood before breaking it to her?

The hostess led them through the busy lunchtime crowd to a reserved table with a good view of the bay. Shawn pulled out a white lattice armchair to seat her.

Such personal service, Lisa thought, taking in his charming manner and the beautiful view. *Does he do this for every woman he meets or is he simply flattering me to make a good impression?*

As soon as he seated her, a female server appeared to take their drink orders. "Would you like a glass of wine before lunch?"

"No, thank you." She smiled. "I would like a glass of water instead, please."

"Bring us a couple bottles of water and lime wedges," Shawn said and eased into his chair.

Lisa: Beach Brides Series

"Thank you for inviting me for lunch," Lisa said, unfolding her napkin. "This is my first time at this restaurant, but I've heard many compliments about the food from our guests."

"Have you lived on the island all your life?"

"No," she said as she clasped her hands together in her lap. "I've only been a resident for about fifteen months. I moved here from Florida to help my aunt operate her bed and breakfast hotel, Bella's Enchanted B&B, in Morganville."

A serving assistant arrived at their table and deposited a basket of warm rolls with butter.

Shawn pulled back the cloth over the rolls and offered her one. "Why did you decide to leave Florida and move here? That's quite a change of pace—from Disneyworld to Morganville."

Lisa laughed, finding it easy to talk to him in spite of her wariness. "As a kid, I used to come here for vacations with my family. I've always loved this place." She selected a roll and pulled it apart. "I recently spent some time here on vacation with friends and came a couple days early to visit with my aunt," she said as she spread whipped butter on each half of her roll. "When Elsie asked me to help her manage the B&B, I initially turned her down but when I returned to the states, things unexpectedly fell into place, making it the right choice."

"Do you like being your own boss?"

Denise Devine

She thought about the day she returned to work after vacation to find out the company had shut down the office. Ten years of service—wiped out within moments. "Elsie is still the boss, but yes, I love the freedom I have now. I get up early because I want to. I work hard because I love what I do."

Their server appeared with the water and silently set it on the table.

"Any regrets?"

"Not one." She sipped her water and decided to change the subject. Shawn had been asking all of the questions. It was her turn. "How about you, Shawn? How do you like your job?"

"I'm in a similar situation." The tiny lines around his mouth tightened, indicating she may have touched upon a sensitive subject. "My father owns the corporation and he still calls the shots, but I like taking over a hotel and running my own show."

The server set their salad plates on the table, a mixture of greens garnished with papaya slices and drizzled with sweet ginger vinaigrette.

Lisa picked up her fork and speared a piece of lettuce. "How long do you plan to remain on Enchanted Island?"

He looked up. "I'm going back to the states as soon the project is finished."

"Isn't spending so much time on the road

difficult for your family?"

An odd light flickered in his hazel eyes. "I'm not in a relationship right now, but you're right; it isn't easy to travel for work for long periods of time and maintain a normal life."

"I would imagine so."

"Do you have time to take a short walk after lunch?" he asked changing the subject. "I'd like to view the site with you and discuss the architectural plans."

Their lunch arrived while he was still speaking. The server set a long white platter in front of her containing a small, crab-stuffed lobster tail, two jumbo Cruzan garlic shrimp and grilled vegetables.

She laughed. "I'll definitely need to get some exercise after eating this much food!"

After that, their discussion veered toward lighter subjects while they enjoyed their meal. Lisa passed on dessert, ordering a rich cup of freshly ground coffee instead.

The Regis property line ran parallel to the Amaryllis Hotel's boundary. Lisa and Shawn left the restaurant and walked through the hotel lobby to the front plaza then crossed the gravel service road that separated the Amaryllis from the vacant property.

"Gosh, it looks so different now," Lisa said,

feeling sad as she scanned the empty acreage. "This entire area used to be dense forest. It's a shame to destroy such natural beauty for a strip mall." She pointed toward a narrow dirt trail that led to a rocky slope. "My cousins and I used to take this path down to the ocean. We weren't supposed to be on this side of the island, much less near the water without adult supervision, but that never stopped us." She grinned mischievously. "We were looking for pirate treasure."

Shawn grinned back. "Did you find any?"

"Ha-ha! We'd all be rich now if we had!"

They walked the length of the property, discussing the layout of the mall. Shawn pointed out the area where a stairway would lead to a long dock and a new stop for the water taxi.

"You do know what's on the other side of this land, don't you?"

He shrugged. "A privately-owned forest, I guess."

"It's ten square miles of forest, beaches and natural caves that, until recently, was owned by Anna LaBore," Lisa said as they walked along. "She died about a year ago—at ninety-seven—and left her entire estate in a trust to the Island Preservation Commission. The land had been handed down from generation to generation in her family since the 1860s."

Shawn stared at her in surprise. "What is the

commission planning to do with it?"

"Oh, Anna left specific instructions on what she wanted the commission to do with her plantation," she said as she stepped over a couple flat rocks, "and she also left them her fortune to carry it out. Her home is currently undergoing restoration as a museum. It still has much of the original furnishings."

"Really?" He stopped and gazed across the Regis land to the dense tropical forest on the LaBore property. "I'd like to see that."

"Are you interested in history?" At his nod, she added, "The interior is in good shape, but the restoration team is still in the process of painting, upgrading the utilities and cataloging everything. It won't be open for a couple months."

The excitement in his eyes dimmed. "I'll probably be back in the states by then."

They turned and began walking back to the hotel. "I've got an idea," Lisa said, hoping her offer didn't come across as a hair-brained scheme. "The place is fenced off to discourage gawkers from driving onto the property, and it sits on top of a hill so it's visible for miles, but I know where there is a secret entrance. If you want to see the restoration in progress I can get you in after hours and show you around."

"Aren't you worried about getting caught?" He

frowned. "What if we trip an alarm? I'd hate to get arrested for trespassing."

"This is Enchanted Island," she replied with a wry chuckle. "There aren't any alarms and we won't get arrested. But we do have to be discreet and that's why I suggested we use a specific entrance. Aunt Elsie is on the commission and she'd be upset if word got around that someone saw me snooping about the place without the commission's permission."

Her sandal suddenly slipped on loose sand covering a flat rock. She screamed, dreading the embarrassment of falling flat on her butt like a klutz. Before she hit the ground, however, Shawn's strong arms caught her and held her tight. In her panic, she threw her arms around his neck. Her soft cheek brushed the rough edge of his jaw, the bold scent of his cologne filled her nostrils.

He went still, holding her close.

"Thank you...for...catching me," she said as she gazed into his eyes, barely aware that she'd spoken. She pulled her arms away and placed her palms against his broad, muscular chest.

"I didn't want you to get hurt." His throaty voice trailed off on a flat note, making him sound distracted.

She couldn't look away, mesmerized by the tiny dimple in his chin, the softness in his hazel eyes. "We—we'd better get going. I told my aunt I'd be home by check-in time."

He gently let go of her and glanced at his sport watch. "It's almost three now." He grabbed her hand and began to walk her back to the hotel. "I'll give you a ride."

She didn't object. Eating a large lunch had made her tired and the thought of riding in a nice comfortable car rather than a windy, bumpy, taxi ride sounded heavenly.

Shawn didn't say much on the short ride to the B&B and she wondered if he had second thoughts about going to the LaBore plantation or asking her to lunch today. She never meant to end up in his arms and hoped he didn't think she'd deliberately slipped to force their close encounter. Some women did such things to attract men, but not her.

He pulled off the narrow road into the driveway of her house. Shifting the car into Park, he stared straight ahead as though deep in thought.

"Thank you for the ride. I appreciate it." She grabbed her purse and placed her hand on the door latch, anxious to jump out and disappear into the house.

"So, did you mean that about getting inside the LaBore plantation? Do you really know of a secret entrance, or is it just a hole in the fence?"

"Yeah, I meant every word I said," she countered, letting the snappy tone of her voice inform him that she hadn't told him about it to brag or lie. "The secret entrance isn't anywhere near a fence. It's the opening of a cave."

He turned toward her, his eyes widening with amazement. "Really? That sounds exactly like my kind of fun." Flashing a wide grin, he leaned over and held up his palm for a high-five. "Lisa, you're on. What time do you want me to pick you up?"

His sudden reaction wasn't at all what she had expected, but it didn't disappoint. She smacked palms with him and opened the door then slid out of the car. "Be back here at noon tomorrow," she said, leaning inside to give him brief instructions. "We'll have the plantation to ourselves because the restoration crew doesn't work on Saturday. Since it gets dark early now, we're going to need time to view the house and make it back through the woods before the sun goes down. Bring a good flashlight and make sure your phone is fully charged."

She started to shut the door, thought better of it and leaned in again. "Oh, and wear jeans and heavy duty tennis shoes, preferably dark-colored."

"It's starting to sound more like a secret mission than a field trip."

She raised one brow. "You'll see."

She shut the door for good this time and walked slowly into the house, watching him back out and drive away.

Lisa: Beach Brides Series

It's only a trip to explore the LaBore plantation—not a date, she thought to herself. *I want to see what progress they've made anyway and it'll be fun showing it to Shawn.*

Still, she couldn't deny how her heart fluttered at the thought of climbing through a dark cave with Shawn Wells.

****

Shawn didn't get around to checking his personal email account until the following morning. When he did, he received a nice surprise.

Dear City Boy,

I never lie, I'll tell you why, I think it's a waste of time.

I'd like a wedding ring, but I have no such thing, too many mountains to climb.

The bottle wasn't cheap, but it's yours to keep. The story behind the message is funny.

If we ever meet, no fact will I delete, and you'll laugh at this silly bunny.

Island Girl

He shot off a quick reply and closed out his email.

Glancing at his watch, he realized he only had three hours to get everything wrapped up here, change clothes and drive over to Lisa's place. He wished he could leave now. The prospect of exploring that old house intrigued him, but the cave sounded downright thrilling. He'd never met a woman who held an interest in so many of the same things he did.

Whistling an off-key tune, he set out for his first meeting in Pete's office to examine the bids for the mall. Two developers had responded to their request for a proposal.

His good mood didn't last long. His phone began to ring and when he pulled it from his pocket, the screen showed "W. Wells."

He drew in a tense breath. "Hey, Dad, what's up?"

"How many bids did you receive?"

Shawn winced. His father sounded as cheerless as ever. "Pete said two came in by the deadline."

"That's all? Start again. You need more."

"Yeah, but Dad, we haven't even looked at these yet. They're from reputable companies."

"Who are they?"

Shawn recited the names of the companies who had responded. Both were from Miami. Having worked with both developers in the past, Wyn rejected them for various reasons that made no sense to Shawn.

"Dad, I'm on my way to Pete's office right now

to review them. Let me look at them first."

Wyn practically cut him off, giving him orders to "cast the net wider" and solicit more proposals. Wyn's bullishness made him wonder if many of the reputable developers in the states simply didn't want to do business with him any longer.

"Look, I don't see the point in trashing these bids before we evaluate them," Shawn said, trying to stay calm. "If neither are within our budget and timeframe, maybe we should rethink the strip mall idea. Maybe we need to look at the concept of timeshares or honeymoon villas. That property has a lot of potential. It sits next to a reserve—"

"Stick with the plan, son. That's what I sent you to do."

Shawn rubbed the back of his neck, becoming agitated at the domineering tone of Wyn's voice. "Why are you so set on building these shops?"

"The resorts on Enchanted Island bring in a lot of well-heeled tourists and they're going to spend their money somewhere. We need to capitalize on those dollars."

"Dad, I just don't think there is a large enough market on this island for so much retail. I saw the changes in the proposal. It looks like you're deliberately going head-to-head with the merchants in Morganville to put them out of business."

"That's right."

He couldn't believe it. Why did they have to resort to such an aggressive tactic? He thought of the women who had protested on the plaza. They were good, decent people with families to feed. "No, that's not right, Dad. I'm not going to deliberately destroy those businesses—"

"Look if you can't do the job I sent you to do," Wyn said, his voice steely calm, "I'll find someone who can."

Shawn stopped in front of Pete's office.

He's threatening me. My own father is threatening me...

He suddenly began to wonder if he even *wanted* to do this job any longer. Pleasing his father had long ago become an exercise in futility. Wyn's imperious "my way or the highway" attitude was the main reason he'd left New York City and worked his way around the country taking on the hotels in the Wells Corporation that weren't turning a decent profit and reviving them. He liked being his own boss and couldn't see how Ian could handle the stress of working so closely with their father, putting up with his callousness and iron grip on the business day in and day out. Ian, obviously, had a lot more patience than he did. He almost felt sorry for his older brother. Almost.

Finding himself cut out of the Desert Indigo project and being the last to know had been a turning point for him, though at the time, the news had shocked and hurt him so deeply, he hadn't realized it. He did now, though, because it had been weighing heavily on his mind ever since.

He heard Wyn bellowing in his ear and realized he'd tuned out the old man a while ago.

"I'm sorry, Dad. I must have a bad connection. I'll call you back."

He cut off the call and shoved the phone deep in his pants pocket. Sure, he'd call Wyn back, sometime next week...

Chapter Five

"I'LL TAKE MY lunch to the shop," Elsie said carrying a small plate holding a sandwich made with her homemade bread. "You have a nice time now." She stopped and quizzically examined Lisa's outfit. "You're wearing that? Where are you going, hiking?"

Lisa had squeezed into a pair of black stretch jeans and a camo T-shirt to blend in with the foliage. She didn't want to risk the possibility of anyone seeing them walk through the woods or enter the cave. Instead of carrying a purse, she'd strapped on her hip pack and stuffed it with her phone, her driver's license and a small wad of cash for emergencies. "Yeah, sort of."

The jingling of a small bell on the gift shop's door echoed through the house, indicating a customer had entered the store to browse.

"Well, have a good time, but be careful about climbing on jagged rocks if you're going out to hike along the coast," Elsie called over her shoulder on her way to greet her customer.

Lisa sat at her computer and opened up the

email program to see if she'd received a message from "City Boy." When she saw it, her heart tapped a little dance. She clicked on it and read the latest poem, but sighed, disappointed that he didn't want to exchange them any longer.

Dear Island Girl,

I think we should meet. Which island do you call home?

A public place would be nice, or at least chat on the phone.

May we talk without a rhyme? Dr. Seuss needs to quit yakking, he's in my head all the time.

City Boy

It's fun, but not practical, she thought to herself. *It's time to get real.*

She opened a new email and wrote:

Dear City Boy,

You're right; we should meet. The poems are fun, but we need to have an old-fashioned conversation and find out if we have more in common than talking like Dr. Seuss. I live on Enchanted Island. Where do you live? Perhaps we can find a midway point.

Oh, and one more question I've been meaning to ask. Are you over 18? Because if you aren't, this conversation stops right now. I'm thirty-three. How old are you?

Island Girl (For security purposes, I'm not revealing my name until we see each other in person.)

There...she'd posed some serious questions. She had no intention of giving out any more information about herself until she'd received satisfactory answers. She sent the email and closed out the program. It was nearly noon. Shawn would be here any minute.

She gathered her long, dark hair into a ponytail as she paced through the house, nervous and excited at the same time. She'd never shown anyone the secret entrance to Anna's mansion. Could she trust Shawn to keep this information to himself? So far, she had no reason to believe she couldn't.

The clock in the kitchen struck the hour twelve times. She glanced out the window at the empty street. What had happened to Shawn? Was he operating on *island time,* or had he simply changed his mind?

Ten minutes later, she heard tires crunching on the driveway. Grabbing her long, blue flashlight, she hurried out of the house. Shawn had barely come to a stop before she'd jerked open the door of his Jeep Renegade and jumped into the passenger seat. "Hi!"

He looked ready for action in a black Miami Dolphins cap, a gray Henley and dark cargo pants, but his grim expression caused him to appear more apprehensive than excited.

"What's the matter? Have you changed your mind?"

He pulled a pair of metal-rimmed sunglasses from the center console and slipped them on. "Nope. It's been a challenging day, but it just got a lot better." Grinning, he shifted the car in reverse and backed out of the driveway. "Lead the way."

Lisa pointed in the direction he'd come. "That way. Back to the Amaryllis."

They parked the Renegade in the hotel parking lot and took the path through the Regis property down to the beach. They walked along the sand for several miles, climbing over jagged rocks and thick foliage.

At one point, Shawn stopped and stared at the rugged terrain. "Are you sure you know where we're going?"

She laughed and tugged on the bill of his cap. "It's not much farther. We have to climb this bank and walk along the cliff for a while."

They scaled the steep bank and walked along the edge of the rock, staring down at the clear aqua water several stories below. Lisa stopped and drew in a deep breath, taking in the fresh ocean air. She loved it up here. In the distance, Anna's majestic yellow house with white gingerbread trim sat in full view. She turned and began to climb the steep terrain into the forest.

Denise Devine

They eventually came to a large, craggy opening in an outcrop of rock. Rays of sun peaked through the tops of the trees, providing a shower of filtered light into the hole.

"It's right here." Lisa turned on her flashlight and went in first. Stepping carefully, she bent at the waist with one hand holding the light, the other grasping the rough wall for support. Slowly she descended the jagged, rocky slope that led down into the cave. "Watch your step. The rocks can be slippery. There's a rough path worn in the slope from foot traffic, but you still have to be careful or you could slip and fall."

They descended into the cool, dark cave until the path leveled out.

Lisa stopped and flashed her light around a large cavern. "Anna told me once this cave goes on for miles. If you go that way," she said and turned around, pointing the beam of her flashlight past the opening to where the cave curved in the opposite direction, "it goes all the way to the ocean. There's a huge opening down in the bay so large you can hide a boat in it. Years ago, her family used to store rum in here. They made a fortune selling it to the states during Prohibition." She pointed the flashlight downward to show him where the sand-covered path split and veered off into opposite directions. She gestured toward the left. "We're going that way."

They walked a short distance on the damp,

uneven ground then encountered another incline. High-pitched squeaking sounds echoed above their heads.

Shawn stopped behind her. "What's that noise?"

She turned around and flashed the light toward the high ceiling. "It's just a few bats. Don't worry, they won't bother us."

They followed the path upward through a narrow opening chipped in the rock that led them into a manmade tunnel.

Shawn flashed a ray of light along the low ceiling, examining the huge wooden beams. "How did you find this place?"

"My cousins and I used to come with Aunt Elsie to visit Anna. We spent hours combing through the woods and playing down by the shore. One day we came across the opening by accident. The next day we snuck back here with flashlights and explored the interior."

"How old were you?"

She kept her light focused on the ground, careful not to trip on loose rocks along the way. "Oh, probably ten."

"You weren't afraid to climb down into a dark hole?"

The amazement in his voice made her laugh.

"Uh-uh. Why would I be afraid? I was with my cousins. Back then, we had no conception of danger. Oh, we knew better than to tell Elsie about it, though. She would have had a heart attack on the spot—that is, after she gave us all a good lesson with a switch. We all swore to keep our discovery a secret." She smiled to herself. "And everyone did—except me. Years later, I shared my little tale with Anna. That's when she told me about her family making and selling rum during the Roaring Twenties. She also scolded me for being so reckless and told me not to go into the cave anymore." She automatically shrugged, even though she knew he couldn't see it in the dark. "But I did anyway. I couldn't resist the temptation to explore."

She thought of something else and turned around abruptly, splaying her hand on the center of Shawn's chest to prevent him from crashing into her. The flashlight dangled in her hand, casting its light at their feet. "Most people laugh at the notion, but I think there is a good possibility of pirate treasure hidden on the island."

"Now, why do you believe that?" he replied, his voice threaded with amusement.

The heat of his chest warmed her palm, distracting her as it rose and fell with each breath. The crown of her head brushed his chin, making her realize how close they were, but she couldn't seem to move away. "Just ask any of the old timers on the island about it and they'll talk your ear off," she

Lisa: Beach Brides Series

blurted in an effort to keep her mind off his nearness. "They swear this island was overrun with pirates back in the day because of all the huge caves and the fact that it was uninhabited."

"So, you want to hunt for pirate treasure," he murmured in a deep, sexy voice. His palm deftly slid across her shoulder and rested on the nape of her neck. "That's an adventure for another day, isn't it?"

The gentle touch of his hand sent a tremor down her spine. When she lifted her chin, his face was a mere silhouette in the shadowy light cast by the flashlights. His lips were a breath away from hers.

Something scurried past their feet, startling her. "What was that?" She tried to move out of its way, but instead, bumped into the damp wall.

Shawn took her by the arm and gently turned her in the right direction. "I think we'd better get going."

They continued walking through the dark tunnel, ducking under spider webs and occasionally hearing odd sounds. Eventually they came to a wooden door.

Lisa pointed her flashlight at it. "This is it."

Shawn stood close behind her. "Where are we?"

"We're at the house." She pulled up on the metal latch and pushed on the door. It wouldn't

Denise Devine

budge. She pushed harder to no avail. "Oh, no. I hope the workers haven't sealed it."

Suddenly, Shawn's large hands were on each side of her pressing on the damp, wooden structure. His body leaned so close she could feel his heart beating and hear him breathing in her ear. She moved aside as he braced his shoulder against it and pushed hard. It moved slightly. They both pushed again. It creaked loudly when it finally gave way, causing them to stumble into a small storage room in the cellar. The door served as the backside of movable shelves.

"This door badly needs its hinges oiled," Lisa said as she pushed the shelving back into place until she heard the latch click. "Come on, let's go upstairs."

The huge house, built on the top of a hill, had a lower level, a main level, an upper floor and an attic. They took the stairs to the main level and walked into a wide, but empty interior courtyard in the center of the building. Lisa stood silently, allowing Shawn a few moments to take in the old-world grandeur of the setting. His eyes flared with astonishment at the two-story room with red brick flooring and Roman Tuscan columns made of stone. The second floor had a decorative wrought iron railing around the entire perimeter. Sunlight flooded through the "lunette" or half-moon-shaped windows above the doorways lining the balcony.

"Anna used to have dozens of potted plants

down here lined up between the columns. The one thing I remember most about this room is the natural brightness and the greenery." She glanced around. The light-colored walls were freshly painted, but bare. She assumed the commission had removed the portraits of Anna's ancestors for cleaning and not taken them down permanently. She made a sweeping motion with her hand. "This courtyard leads to several individual parlors, the library, the dining room and a great room. What do you want to see first?"

He chose the library and she led him into a corner room with heavy, ornate floor-to-ceiling shelves filled with antique books, brightly upholstered sofas and Persian rugs. They systematically walked through every room, peeking under the dust covers to view the furnishings. Some rooms were finished; others were empty and undergoing restoration. Painting equipment, ladders and other items were scattered throughout the house where the workers were finishing their tasks.

They took the stairs, decorated with the same style of ornate wrought iron railing as the balcony in the inner courtyard, to the second floor to view the bedrooms. Up there, they opened Anna's bedroom door, walked past a dark, four-poster bed and opened the double, French-paned doors to a wide veranda. Scaffolding encased the entire back of the house for painting, but they were still able to get a good look at the gently sloping landscape dotted with palms and in the distance, the calm, aqua waters of the Caribbean. Light, puffy clouds drifted lazily across the blue sky.

Shawn leaned against the railing and gazed across the property. "I can't imagine what it must have been like to live here. This place is like a...a tropical castle."

She stood next to him, wondering what it would be like to live here with him, just the two of them, wandering through this huge house together and discovering all of its secrets. "Anna was born here and lived here for ninety-seven years. She loved it so much she rarely left the premises. I can understand why she wanted it preserved forever."

"You were fortunate to have known her." He slid his arm around her shoulders and pulled her close. "Thank you for bringing me here. It was well worth the risk of letting you drag me through a damp, bat-infested cave."

She laughed. "Don't forget about the snakes and spiders."

"You're the first—no—the *only* female I've ever known who didn't go all ballistic over that stuff."

"Why bother?" She shrugged. "It's a fact of life around here."

He smiled and squeezed her shoulder, dipping his face close to hers. "You're amazing." His gaze dropped to her lips and her pulse began to race.

She lifted her head, sensing his intent to kiss her—

The jarring sound of a car door slamming jerked her back to reality. She gasped and pulled away. "Did you hear that?"

Shawn looked puzzled. "No, hear what?"

Then they both heard it.

"Someone is here!"

"I thought you said no one would be here today!"

With Shawn on her heels, Lisa shut the veranda doors and tore out of Anna's bedroom. "There shouldn't be anyone here but us."

She ran along the balcony to the other side of the house into a front bedroom to look out the window. "Oh, my gosh."

Two late model cars had pulled into the driveway and three people were standing in front of the house gazing up at the exterior.

Lisa pulled back, worried they might see her. "It looks like a couple council members and the president of the Island Preservation Commission. We have to get out of here *now*. Elsie would die of embarrassment if I got caught sneaking around."

Their tennis shoes pounded on the wooden flooring as they ran to the stairway and thundered down the stairs. Lisa came to an abrupt stop at the bottom and peered through the courtyard. "Oh, no, they're at the front door." She cut a sharp right through an arched doorway and sprinted through a small, empty parlor to a back stairway.

"Where are we going? This isn't the way we came."

Voices echoed through the house as the new arrivals entered the courtyard through the front door.

"We're going leave by the kitchen," she whispered. "It's in the rear of the house. There's no time to go back through the tunnel. They might see us cutting through the courtyard. Besides, that door in the cellar made enough noise to wake the dead." She waved her hand. "Follow me!"

She crept slowly down the stairs to keep the creaking of the old wood to a minimum. At the bottom, Lisa ran into a long, narrow kitchen filled with wall-to-wall cupboards, scarred wooden countertops and a large cast iron stove. She slowly pulled open the back door and waited for Shawn to exit then shut it quietly behind her.

They ran across the grounds behind the house, not stopping until they were on a footpath that led into the woods.

Once they were out of sight, they collapsed on the ground, laughing like a couple of errant teenagers.

"You're crazy," Shawn managed to say between gasps of breath. "Do you realize how close we came to getting caught?"

"I've been here several times on a Saturday and I've never encountered a soul," she said, wiping stray wisps of hair from her brow as she lay on her back. "I wish we'd had more time. There were many things I didn't have the chance to show you, like the secret staircase to the attic. You'd be surprised at all the unique nooks and crannies my cousins and I discovered about this place."

Shawn propped himself up on one elbow. "Do me a favor and stay out of that cave unless I'm with you, okay? Our phones didn't work in there. I checked. If something happened and you couldn't make it back out, no one would know where to look for you."

"Except *you*." She made a face at his request then switched to a mischievous grin. "Does that mean you plan to do this with me again?"

He leaned over her and looked searchingly into her eyes. "Do you *want* me to come back here with you again?"

"Yes," she said, the word escaping her lips in barely a whisper. "I'd love for you...and me..."

"This is the most fun I've had in a long time. I know that sounds clichéd, but it's true. I enjoy being with you, Lisa, and I know you feel the same way." He slid his arm around her waist, drawing her toward him.

Denise Devine

She knew she should deny it and push him away, but his words had awakened the lonely little girl inside her. Yes, she did enjoy being with him—too much and it left her vulnerable to getting her heart broken again.

He lifted his hand to her face, his smooth fingertips brushing her cheek. Her breath caught in her throat as he slid his palm behind her head and pulled her toward him, placing a tender kiss on her lips. The sweet pressure of his mouth on hers made her pulse race, awaking desires that she had tucked away in her heart months ago.

She circled her arms around his neck and breathed in his scent, feeling the strength of his arms surrounding her, the warmth of his skin against hers.

His arms tightened around her, pulling her close as they deepened the kiss. "I've wanted to do this ever since yesterday," he murmured, "when you fell into my arms." He pulled back and smiled. "I've never had that happen before."

Her face grew warm at the thought. "I didn't do it on purpose, I swear."

He smiled. "I'm glad you did, though."

A long snake slithered across the trail. They froze, waiting for it to go on its way.

She sat up. "We'd better get going. We've got some heavy duty walking to do."

Shawn stood, then reached down and took her by the hand, helping her to her feet. "Since we're not going back through the cave, how do we get out of here?"

"Through a hole in the fence," she said wryly. "This trail leads to the road. We can take it all the way back to the hotel, but we need to hurry. I don't want to run into those council members on their way driving back to town. I'm sure they didn't see us running across the grounds, but this road is private. It cuts through the heart of Anna's property and seeing us walking along might make them question what we're doing here. Let's go."

"Fine with me." He glanced around cautiously. "I don't want to be in or near this forest when it starts getting dark."

They walked along the narrow trail through the dense forest until the path intersected with the road. Lisa pointed to a spot where a car had gone into the ditch and damaged the fence. They stepped over the torn metal fabric and jogged back to the Amaryllis.

"I'm beat," Lisa said once they arrived at the hotel. "I need to go home and take a shower."

They were silent on the ride back to her house. She'd begun to have second thoughts about kissing him and wondered if he had, too. They'd only known each other a few days and given the fact that she still opposed his development on the Regis property, the situation between them could grow uncomfortable in the near future, both personally and professionally. She didn't want to put herself in the middle between Shawn and the women in her business league, not now—not ever.

He stopped the car in her driveway and leaned over to kiss her goodbye, but she pulled away. "I don't think this is a good idea, Shawn. Given the situation we're in professionally and the fact that you're only staying temporarily, it might be best if we simply remained friends."

Disappointment clouded his eyes, but she knew by his silence that he understood they had both made an error in judgment. "All right, Lisa. If that's what you want."

"It's how we need to proceed." She opened the car door. "Goodbye, Shawn."

She heard his car pull away as she walked in the house, but she didn't turn around and wave goodbye. She didn't want him to see the sadness she knew mirrored in her eyes.

****

On Monday morning, Shawn sat at his desk, bouncing his pen on his note pad as he mulled over Lisa's desire to remain friends *only*. It had disappointed him, but he respected her decision and understood he needed to let it go. In a few months, Wyn would turn the hotel over to a new manager and

Lisa: Beach Brides Series

he'd head back to the states. Getting involved with Lisa would simply complicate matters.

Why, then, did it bother him so much?

He booted up his computer and typed the password to access his email. His Internet "pen pal," Island Girl, had replied to his previous message. As he read it, he decided to set up a place and time to meet her.

He created a new email document and began to type:

Dear Island Girl,

You raise some valid questions. I assure you, I'm well over eighteen years old. I'm actually thirty-five. I also live on Enchanted Island, so deciding on a neutral place to meet will be easy and convenient for both of us.

Are you familiar with the establishment next to the Hideaway Cove Resort—Nigel's Bar and Grill? If so, is next Wednesday night at eight o'clock convenient? If you aren't comfortable meeting there, feel free to pick another place.

You shouldn't have any trouble recognizing me; I'll be wearing a red shirt.

Waiting to hear from you,

City Boy

To his surprise, within five minutes, he received a reply.

Denise Devine

Dear City Boy,

Yes, I'm available on Wednesday evening and I'm very comfortable with meeting at Nigel's. I know the owner and can vouch that he makes the best conch chowder on the island.

A red shirt? Sounds like a good plan. I'll wear a red ribbon in my hair.

See you then,

Island Girl

Happy to be able to finally meet this woman, he closed his email and locked his computer, aware that he had to get some work done today.

He wanted to go to Morganville with Pete to look around the business district. He needed to see firsthand what types of vendors had established shops there so he didn't duplicate them when leasing space in the mall. But he couldn't simply wander along Main Street, staring through shop windows and asking nosy questions. Knowing how the island gossip network operated, his presence would probably create the impression that he was gathering ammunition to shut them down. He'd concluded that he needed someone reputable from the island to give him a tour and he only knew one person who could fill that role.

A half-hour later, he stood at the front door of Bella's Enchanted Bed and Breakfast Hotel, hoping to catch Lisa at home. She answered the door wearing white jean shorts and a pink top with puffy sleeves and a ruffled neckline.

"Hi," she said sharply, sounding as though she found his presence uncomfortable.

"May I come in?" The grim expression on her face made him wonder if he'd made a mistake. Maybe they weren't even friends any longer.

She stood back and opened the door, allowing him to pass. He walked into a large room filled with lemon-colored walls, white wicker furniture with lavender and yellow cushions and matching accent tables.

"I didn't expect to see you again," she said, shutting the door behind him. "If this is about our conversation the other night—"

"No, it's not. I was wondering if you would give me a tour of Main Street. I'd like to get a feel for the businesses that are operating there and since you're the spokesperson for the business league, I figured you'd be the best person to show me around."

"Why don't you ask Shakara? She's the president."

"Pete is probably talking to her right now. We thought if we were seen with the two of you, the shopkeepers would be more open to talking with us."

Her jade eyes filled with skepticism. "Is that the only reason you're here?"

The knowing look in her eyes revealed she knew the truth.

He wanted to take her in his arms and hold her close, but instead let them fall to his sides. "I wanted to see you again, too."

"Shawn, we can't—"

"As friends, I mean." He held up his hands in a gesture of peace. "I need your help on this, Lisa. Say you'll do it, please."

She sighed. "I'm sorry, but I can't. My aunt had an appointment this morning so I can't leave. One of us always has to be here."

"Will she be long?"

"She had a few things to pick up on her way home, but said she should be back by noon."

He checked his sport watch. "It's close to noon now. Mind if I wait?"

"It's up to you." She pointed toward the sofa. "Have a seat while I pour some Switchta."

She disappeared into the kitchen, her bare feet padding softly on the tiled floor. He made himself comfortable on the sofa, taking in the cheery feel of the room. When she returned, he asked her how they came up with the name "Bella's Enchanted B&B."

"Aunt Elsie named the hotel after her youngest daughter, Bella," Lisa said as she handed him a tumbler. "She had always planned to turn it over to her daughter someday, but Bella decided island life was too boring and the demands of a small business too much work. She followed her three older siblings to the states, leaving Elsie to run the business by herself. That's why Elsie made an offer to me. I said 'yes,' found a buyer for my townhouse and have been here ever since." She set her glass on a coaster on the wicker coffee table. "Would you like to see the house? The rooms are empty and clean. Check-in time isn't until three o'clock."

He shrugged. "Sure."

She took him through the six bedrooms on the upper level, explaining how they had painted and decorated each room in a different color and had given each room the name of its color. The lower level had originally contained three bedrooms for private use, but after her children left home, Elsie had turned the third bedroom into a consignment gift shop to bring in extra income.

Touring the house made him realize all that she would lose if the business went bankrupt and it made him uneasy about the development at the Amaryllis. The shops needed to complement the downtown merchants to bring more people to the island to shop, not to compete.

A bell jingled in a rear room of the house. "I'm back," Elsie said, her voice echoing from the kitchen.

"I'm in the living room, Auntie," Lisa said and

Denise Devine

stood, collecting the empty glasses.

Elsie came into the doorway of the living room holding a sack of groceries. The moment she saw Shawn, her eyes narrowed with distrust.

"This is Shawn Wells, Auntie. The manager of the Amaryllis."

Elsie and Shawn exchanged greetings.

"Shawn wants me to walk downtown with him and show him around. We're going to meet with Shakara, too."

"Huh," Elsie said and went into the kitchen. "Suit yourself."

Lisa excused herself to put on her sandals and grab her purse while Shawn waited by the door. Elsie came back into the living room with several wedges of pastry on a plate. Her sudden hospitality took him by surprise. "Have a slice of coconut tart, Mr. Wells. I make it fresh for breakfast every day. It's my specialty."

The words sounded more like an order than a polite request, so Shawn thanked her and helped himself. The golden, doughy tart resembled a lattice-topped cake, but when he took a bite, the sweet flavor of coconut melted in his mouth. He wished they made this at the hotel.

Lisa returned with her purse slung over her shoulder. "I'll be back by three, Auntie."

Lisa: Beach Brides Series

They left the house and walked past a small island park and a few residential houses as they made their way toward Main Street. Once there, Shawn stared in dismay. He'd expected a quaint two-block area of colorful historic buildings. What he saw caused him to pause. Instead of a vibrant shopping mall rich with character and unique shops, he found a deserted street, weeds and rampant neglect. The facades of the buildings were faded, some crumbling. The sidewalks were cracked and uneven in places. The cobblestone street needed tearing up and repaving reusing the same blocks to preserve its historic integrity. A couple old light posts stood forlornly on the street corners, but he couldn't tell if they even operated any longer. A few tourists walked about, but carried very few purchases.

No wonder these people are afraid of my development. They don't need competition; they need resuscitation.

Lisa must have sensed his shock. She clutched her purse and avoided looking him in the eyes. He let out a tense breath, completely at a loss as to what to say. He wanted to tell her something positive about his experience, but the words wouldn't come.

"The business league has been working with the island council to fund improvements to the downtown area for a year, but the council keeps delaying a decision," she said suddenly. "It's difficult for the shopkeepers, who have waited patiently so long, to see your development getting so much

Denise Devine

attention."

Across the street, a battered door opened to a small store on the corner and Pete appeared. He waved them over to Shakara's shop.

Pete stood behind the counter with his arm around Shakara as they entered into her place. The postage stamp-sized room held several glass cases filled with stunning pieces of handcrafted jewelry made from semi-precious stones and local shells. The woman had amazing talent, but very little business. It made Shawn sad to see such exceptional artistic skills going to waste.

Shakara didn't seem fazed by it. She smiled and flirted with Pete, seemingly without a care in the world. The hem of her green and white flowered halter dress brushed her ankles as she spun around for Pete. "Does my boongie look good in this dress?"

Pete's eyes twinkled as a wide grin curved his lips. He looked down at her round derrière. "Honey, your boongie looks good in everything."

She burst into a sexy laugh. "Smart bey. I just might keep you 'round for a while."

Pete slid his arm around her waist, pulling her close. Obviously, things had progressed between them faster than Pete had let on.

Shawn opened the door. "Shall we go?"

Lisa and Shakara described each of the shops

they passed by as the four strolled down the street, two by two. They came upon a small barbershop and spoke with the elderly barber, an islander with graying hair and stooped shoulders. The faded pole with red and blue stripes in front of his establishment didn't spin anymore, its rusted casing proof it had hung on the storefront for decades. Farther along, they talked to the owners of a beauty shop, a small clothing shop and several specialty gift shops, including an interesting little shop called Island Antiques.

At the corner, Shawn looked across the street and saw a tall, three-storied structure that appeared abandoned. The shutters had been closed on all of the windows. "This looks interesting." He pointed to it as they stepped off the curb and headed toward it.

"That's the Morganville Hotel," Shakara said. "What's left of it, anyway."

"It closed down about ten years ago," Lisa added.

The faded "flamingo" pink building with white trim had rusting balconies on the second and third floors supported by several large columns. The barely discernable words MORGANVILLE HOTEL 1861 were etched in the façade between the top floors. Shawn walked toward the hotel, wondering what it looked like on the inside. "I wish we could see the rest of it." He stood in front of the building and stared at the upper floors.

"Then go inside." Shakara began to laugh. "This is Enchanted Island, *bey*. Nobody locks their doors here."

Intrigued by the prospect of checking out the interior, Shawn walked into the entryway and tried the front door. *It opened.* Taking Lisa by the hand, he stepped inside. Once his eyes adjusted to the dim light, he found a large lobby area with a grand staircase that led to the second level. Something small and furry scurried across the wooden floor and disappeared in a crack in the wall.

The boards creaked under Shawn's feet as he walked across the room, gazing at the large crystal chandelier in the high ceiling, now dulled by a thick layer of dust and old cobwebs. Though it had fallen into hard times, this hotel had been truly grand back in its heyday.

Outside, Pete and Shakara opened the shutters so light could come through the main windows. Shawn and Lisa spent the next half-hour looking through all of the rooms, opening closet doors and visualizing what the place must have looked like before it closed down. He walked out the back door to find a stone courtyard with a fountain and flower beds, now overgrown with weeds and bougainvillea.

This property has so much potential, he thought wistfully as he walked back inside. *I'd love the challenge of restoring it back to the splendor it once held. I'd love to see the entire downtown restored, too. This place holds so much charm.*

A familiar pang of anxiety plagued his soul and he realized he couldn't work for his father any longer. Sadly, he'd known for a long time he had lost the joy in performing his duties, but he'd kept on doing them anyway. He hadn't wanted to come to this island. Now he saw the good it had done for him. Getting away from everyone had given him a new perspective.

When this job is finished, so am I.

He couldn't wait to get back to the states and into business for himself.

Chapter Six

"I PROMISE TO be home by midnight, and I'll only have one drink. I'm not going to *buss up*," Lisa said, using Shakara's Bahamian slang for "get drunk."

The lines in Elsie's brow deepened with concern as though Lisa had barely reached eighteen instead of thirty-three. "I worry about you going down to Nigel's. That place has had too many police calls." She shook her head. "It's the tourists staying at the resorts causing all the trouble—getting drunk and starting fights. You be careful. Call me when you're leaving and make sure Nigel finds someone to escort you and your friends to your cars. I don't want you girls walking alone through the parking lot after dark."

"I will, Auntie. Don't worry."

Lisa took the keys and headed out to the car. Elsie didn't know she'd been communicating with a total stranger by email and had planned to meet him there. She thought Lisa had coordinated a "girl's night out" with a few people to meet at Nigel's.

I'm over thirty and I can't tell my aunt the

real story about what I'm doing.

Why couldn't she be honest with Elsie? The truth didn't make any sense!

"Is this absolutely the most totally brainless stunt I have ever pulled or what? I should have my head examined." She tossed her wristlet onto the passenger seat, worrying about meeting City Boy. He could be a rapist or a serial killer for all she knew. The thought produced goose bumps on her arms. Maybe she shouldn't go after all...

Wait a minute. This is Enchanted Island, not West Palm Beach. Stop with the scary thoughts.

First of all, she knew Nigel personally and had known him most of her life. He ran a reputable establishment and didn't tolerate troublemakers—which were usually tourists. Second, she had no intention of leaving with "City Boy" and going somewhere alone with him. Third, if he tried anything inappropriate and she resisted, the locals would step in. The most likely scenario, however, would be that she'd meet up with a nice guy and have a good time.

With that thought in mind, she slid in, shoved the key into the ignition and drove out of the driveway.

Elsie had mentioned seeing a clip on the nightly news about a tropical storm brewing. If it stayed on its current path, it would hit the island by the weekend. She breathed a sigh of relief, glad she didn't have to worry about that tonight.

At Nigel's, Lisa stood at the door and scanned the full room, looking for a man in a red shirt. She noticed a group of islanders wearing "rasta tams" over their dreads—crocheted hats with red, green, black and yellow stripes—congregating around a large table in the corner, eating conch chowder and warm Johnny Cake with butter. The aroma hovered in the bar, making her hungry for the chowder, Nigel's signature menu item.

She waved to Nigel behind the rectangular bar. His dark skin glistened under the lights, his graying hair, shorn close to his head, matched his salt and pepper beard. He patted a spot on the bar, signaling he wanted her to take the empty chair. She smiled and sat down, tucking the skirt of her long dress underneath her. She'd worn an ankle-length dress tonight in royal blue with cap sleeves and a round neckline. Shakara had crafted a new jewelry set for her, a heart-shaped pendant made from Larimar on a long sterling silver chain with matching teardrop earrings. The sky-blue gemstone marbled with white contrasted beautifully against the dark fabric of her dress. She'd left her long hair flowing and made a headband out of the red ribbon.

Nigel smiled, revealing a new gold tooth in the front of his mouth. "Ha it go, gyal? Whatcha drinkin'?"

"Hi, Nigel. I'll take a Coke for now. I'm meeting someone here."

"A Coke?" He laughed. "Muddasik dred! You can't ha no fun tha way." He set a wine glass in front of her and filled it with Jamaican Red Label wine. "First one is on da house."

She thanked him and sipped it appreciatively. Perhaps she needed a little wine to settle her nerves. Uncertainty had set in again and worrisome imaginings were getting the best of her.

What if this guy is merely trolling for some hot babe to hop into bed with him?

She shuddered and stared into her wine glass, once again getting second thoughts about this "blind date."

She glanced up and saw a handsome man with short blond hair sitting at the bar wearing a red shirt printed with gold palm fronds. Could he be the one? He looked to be the right age, but she didn't recognize him. If he'd lived on the island for a while, she would have surely seen him somewhere.

He smiled at her. She smiled back. He picked up his drink and walked over, sliding onto the seat of the empty barstool next to her.

"Well, hello there," he said in a deep, sexy drawl.

"Hello, *City Boy*," she replied, hoping he

understood. If not... "I'm *Island Girl*."

"You can call me Darren." His brows rose in amusement, his smile widening. "So, you're Island Girl, huh? What's your real name, or don't you give it out when you're working a place like this?"

What?

Okay, so maybe this guy *wasn't* the right one. Maybe the red shirt was just an unfortunate coincidence...

She clutched her wine glass, ready to bolt at the first sign of trouble. "Are you meeting someone here at eight o'clock?"

"Yeah," Darren said and leaned toward her, sliding his hand across the small of her back. "I've been waiting all night to meet someone like you."

Irritated by his boldness, she pulled his hand away. "Please, don't do that."

"Geez, you're pretty uptight for a girl who came here looking to get picked up."

"Look, I'm not uptight and I didn't come here to get picked up. I'm sorry if I gave you that impression. Now, if you'll excuse me..."

She grabbed her purse and slid off the barstool. "Thanks for the wine," she said to Nigel. He tried to pour her another glass, but she placed her hand over the top of it and shook her head. "I'm leaving." As soon as she got home she planned to delete every email from City Boy and block him, too!

"You're leaving?" Darren stretched out his arm to block her way. "Why, do you want to go somewhere more romantic? All right, let's go." He slid off his barstool and chugged his drink.

She pushed her chair aside and sidestepped him. "Didn't you hear me the first time? I'm leaving, but not with you. *Goodbye.*"

"Ah, come on." He tried to put his arm around her, but she pushed him away. "Look, we'll go to my suite and I'll order Champagne. Strawberries. Chocolate. Whatever it takes, okay?" Obviously, he'd done this sort of thing before. He'd deciphered her refusal as an act to get him to offer her more.

"Stop it." She backed away, ready to shove him if he tried to touch her again. "Get away from me. I'm not going anywhere with you."

From the corner of her eye, she saw Nigel watching, his bushy brows dipping with concern. He pulled his phone from under the bar and dialed 911.

"C'mon, babe." Darren moved close and slid his arms around her. "I'll show you a good time."

She was about to give him a knee in the groin when suddenly a long, powerful arm slid past her and gripped the man by the front of his shirt, lifting him off the floor.

What the...

She turned and saw Shawn glowering at her harasser. He wore a Ralph Lauren polo shirt *in solid red.*

"Get your hands *off* her..."

Darren began to shout colorful curses and swing his fists wildly, but Shawn, having long arms and the advantage of being sober, easily blocked every blow.

Things were happening so fast, Lisa barely got out of the way.

A crowd began to form around the incident, some cheering on the altercation, others trying to break it up.

Shawn shoved Darren away. "Stay away from her or I'll—"

"She came on to me! She's mine!" Darren tried to level a punch to Shawn's face, but Shawn smacked it away.

"Break it up, people. Move aside!" Duane Hall, the police officer on duty tonight—and Nigel's cousin on his mother's side—elbowed his way through the crowd and pulled the men apart. He glared at the drunk. "Ah-ha, so it's *you* again. I warned you about fighting last night and da night before. Now I'm going to lock you up. You're under arrest."

Darren's face turned red and he began to spit

obscenities.

Nigel slipped his phone into the front pocket of his orange flowered shirt. "Duane, how did you get here so fast?"

The husky, island-born cop slapped his cuffs on the drunken man. "I was sitting in my cruiser in da parking lot, waiting for da trouble to start." He shook his finger at Nigel. "You gotta get better customers in dis place. It's a disgrace!"

As an age-old argument between Nigel and Duane ensued, Shawn grabbed Lisa by the hand, pulling her through the barroom and out the back door into the moonless night. Outside, the police cruiser's red and blue lights flashed brightly, looking like a UFO in the parking lot.

"Where are we going," she shouted, running to keep up.

He sounded angry. "Away from here!"

"Wait a minute." She jerked on his hand to make him halt. "Are you *City Boy* or is your red shirt and your appearance in the bar at eight o'clock simply a coincidence?"

He spun around. "What do you think?"

She gasped and snatched her hand away. "Well, if you are, why didn't you tell me this when we first met?"

"I didn't know it myself until I walked into

Nigel's and saw the red ribbon in your hair. I couldn't believe it. Then I saw you getting mauled by a drunken tourist. Whatever possessed you to talk to that jerk?"

"He had a red shirt on," she argued in her own defense. "At first, I thought he was the person who had been emailing me."

"He's a weasel!" Shawn towered over her. "I doubt he's ever read a poem in his life, much less written something that rhymes. You should have seen right through him."

"I did! He wouldn't take no for an answer."

"I can see why." He grabbed her hand and started walking toward the beach. The loud, systematic roar of the waves rushing toward shore and back out to sea should have calmed her, but Shawn's reply made her angrier than before.

"What do you mean by *that*?"

He stopped next to a row of tall palms, their trunks wound with strings of clear lights. "You're beautiful and sexy in that dress. Every guy in the bar couldn't stop looking at you."

She rolled her eyes. "They all know me, Shawn."

"Yeah, and they all want to know you better!"

"What. Is. Your. Problem!"

He grabbed her by the forearms and drew her

close. She tried to pull away by stepping backward, but instead slammed her back against a palm tree.

"You want to know what my problem is?" He drew his face close to hers. "It's simple. I've never been a jealous man, but when I saw you in the bar with that guy and he was trying to put his hands all over you, I had all I could do to keep from ripping his head off." His eyes pierced hers with hurt and confusion. "Look, I know we haven't known each other long, but I don't want to be friends anymore. Do you understand? I want to be *the one*."

She glared at him. "What's the point? It'll only be for a couple months. Once your work is finished, you'll leave the island. Shawn, I won't accept you as a part-time boyfriend. I've already done that once and I'm not going through it again."

His gaze intensified. "Do you think I haven't thought about that? I've got some major decisions to make regarding my future and I promise, when the time comes you'll be with me every step of the way." He pulled the red ribbon out of her hair and let it fly away in the wind. Her silken mane whipped around them like a halo. "Give me a chance, Lisa."

Without waiting for her answer, he crushed his mouth against hers, his arms enveloping her possessively, as though he never wanted to let her go again. The heat of his kiss sent a tremor through her, making her heart race. Wanting more, she slid her hands up his chest and locked them around his neck

Denise Devine

as she pressed her lips to his, melting into him.

Taking her by surprise, he lifted her off her feet and swung her around, lightening the mood and making her laugh. When he set her down, he drew her close again and buried his face in her hair. "Look, I realize it's ridiculous to think I could fall for someone so fast. I don't understand how it happened, but I know what I feel is real. I think about you all the time. I love being with you." He cradled her head in his hands and tipped it upward until their faces were but a breath apart. "I love *you*, Lisa, and I know you love me, too. I can see it in your eyes. I can feel it every time I touch you. There's a connection between us that I've never had with anyone before. I *know* you're the one for me."

She gazed into his eyes, her heart overflowing with happiness. "I thought I knew what love was until I met you, but now I realize it is so much more than I've ever dreamed it could be." She slid her hands over his. "You are *the one for me*, too, Shawn."

"Hey, *Island Girl*," he whispered, "finding that message in a bottle was like winning the lottery. The odds are a hundred million to one, but sooner or later someone gets the winning combo." He smiled and kissed her tenderly on the lips. "This time it was me."

****

Late Friday afternoon, Shawn shut down his computer and cleared off his desk. He'd had a busy day and could have put in more time on the job, but he'd invited Lisa to dinner in the hotel steakhouse and he didn't want to be late. He'd thought about her all day as he sat in staff meetings, dealt with suppliers on the phone and interviewed candidates who'd made the final round for a housekeeping managerial position. No matter what he did, he never let her sweet face stray far from his thoughts.

He'd never been in love before. In the past, he thought he'd experienced it, but his feelings for Brittany—or any woman, for that matter—had never come close to what he had with Lisa. Brittany had done him an immense favor by breaking off her engagement. At the time, he'd taken it hard. He'd come to Enchanted Island angry over the way she'd walked out on him and feeling sorry for himself, but now he knew it had been a great blessing in disguise. Marriage to her would have never lasted.

His phone rang. The caller ID read P. LaMaur.

"Yeah, Pete. What's up?"

"You ready? You hungry? It's ten minutes to five. The girls said they'd meet us in the bar."

Shawn glanced at his sport watch. "Just closing up."

"I'm on my way to your office. Be there in a sec. Bye."

Shawn discontinued the call and looked down, checking his phone for messages. The door to his office opened and shut.

"You must be hungry, LaMaur. That was fast—"

He looked up to find Wyn standing in front of his desk in a navy suit. The surprise rendered him speechless at first, his good mood swiftly plummeting.

"Dad, what are you doing here?" The curt tone in his voice revealed his disappointment. "Why didn't you let me know you were coming?"

The creases in Wyn's face had turned to hard lines. "This isn't a social call."

At that moment, Pete burst in the door. His mouth gaped open so wide his chin nearly bounced off the floor at the site of Wyn's grim, intimidating stance. His gaze nervously bounced from Wyn to Shawn and back to Wyn again. "Did somebody die, er..."

"Close the door, LaMaur. This concerns you, too."

Pete swallowed hard and shut the door.

Shawn sat like a stone, waiting to find out what unpardonable sin he'd committed this time.

Win's jaw clenched. "You're both off this job as of now."

The news hit Shawn like a blow to the chest. He'd never been pulled off a job before.

"Why?" He sprang from his chair. "Everything is rolling along fine. We sent out a new request for proposals a couple days ago."

Wyn's icy blue eyes glittered with an unexplainable anger that always seemed to simmer just below the surface. "Withdraw it. The council has denied our application to build on the Regis property. The project is cancelled." Though he didn't come right out and say it, the sharp edge in his voice clearly insinuated, "*You failed.*"

Pete looked confused. "What happened? Why did the council change their mind?"

Wyn flicked a glance at Pete, but didn't make eye contact. He excelled in letting a person know they were insignificant without saying a single word. "Some old lady who owns a bed and breakfast talked them out of it in a closed-door session on Monday. She got them to agree to revive that slum they call Main Street instead. They didn't formally announce their decision until yesterday or I'd have been here sooner."

So that's where Elsie went on Monday morning, Shawn thought. He remembered her attitude toward him when she returned home. She'd given him a dirty look then offered him her house specialty. An interesting woman. Certainly, a tough one.

Pete's blue eyes widened with alarm. "Wh-what about us?"

Denise Devine

"You're going to Juneau. You leave tonight."

"WHAT?" They both replied at the same time.

Wyn almost smiled and Shawn instinctively knew his father had retaliated with this assignment to Alaska to punish them. "Ian and I flew up there last week and bought a new property," he said sounding extremely satisfied with his accomplishment. "You two need to get it in shape so it's open for business by next spring."

Open for business by next spring?

Shawn exchanged stunned glances with Pete. Then his resolve hardened. This was exactly what he needed to force himself to take the leap and land on his own two feet—where *he* wanted to land.

"I'm not going to Juneau, Dad. Neither is Pete." He'd disagreed with his father many times, but never had he rejected an order outright. The moment caused his nerves to jangle. The exhilaration of breaking free, however, made him wonder why he'd waited so long.

Wyn's eyes narrowed. "You'll go if I say so."

Shawn shook his head. "I quit. I'm through working for you and Ian. Pete and I both are. It's time we started our own corporation."

Wyn let out a mirthless laugh. "You'll fall flat on your face."

"If we do, Mr. Wells," Pete said gravely, "we'll

Lisa: Beach Brides Series

pick ourselves up and start again."

"I've heard enough of this nonsense," Wyn said and walked to the door. "Get your bags packed. We're leaving tonight. You'll catch the red-eye in Miami to Seattle and then a flight tomorrow to Juneau. Your replacement is checking into his room right now." He stopped with his hand on the door. "There's someone waiting for you down in the lounge. I have no doubt she can talk some sense into you."

There's no way Lisa will talk me into moving to Alaska...

Wyn slammed the door shut, leaving Pete and Shawn speechless. Shawn soberly stared at Pete for a moment, letting the enormity of their commitment sink in.

Then they smacked palms together in a high five and cheered.

Chapter Seven

LISA DROVE SHAKARA to the Amaryllis in Elsie's car. The winds of the coming tropical storm had already started to pick up and the water had become somewhat choppy. The taxi was still running, but Lisa and Shakara wanted their hair and makeup to stay fresh for the evening. If any water sprayed into the boat, their clothes would be a mess, too. No taxi for them tonight!

Lisa wore a new dress, a short, stretchy black knit with a round neckline and lacy, elbow-length sleeves. Her gold bib necklace and matching earrings, an exclusive "Shakara" creation, sparkled under the lights.

"I'll meet you in the lounge in a few minutes," Shakara said as they entered the lobby. "Mavis has a check for me." Mavis, the gift shop proprietor, sold an array of Shakara's jewelry on consignment and always made payouts on Friday.

Lisa waved at Shakara and headed for the lounge. She walked in and stared at the special weather report broadcasting on the flat screen TVs mounted behind the bar. "BREAKING NEWS" crawled across the bottom of the screen. TROPICAL STORM MILANA HAS STRENGTHENED INTO A CATEGORY 1 HURRICANE.

Mesmerized, Lisa stood with her arms folded and viewed the newscast. She'd been through tropical storms before, but this was the first time one had turned into a hurricane. If Milana traveled the way the weatherman predicted, Enchanted Island sat right in the middle of its path. She wondered if their house could handle the winds. Aunt Elsie's place had obviously been through this before but...

Something caught her eye and her gaze shifted to a beautiful young blonde in a teal designer dress with matching shoes. The young woman walked into the room with the air of a queen and took a high table near the windows overlooking Azure Bay. Not wanting to appear rude, Lisa pulled out a chair at the bar and tried to get interested in the weather report again, but couldn't help studying her. Something about her seemed out of place.

She looks absolutely perfect, but not perfectly happy. I wonder why.

The bartender, a short, balding man, walked over to the woman's table and placed a cocktail napkin in front of her along with a small carafe of snack mix. "Good evening," he said, greeting the blonde in a cordial manner. "What would you like to drink?"

She placed her patent leather Gucci clutch on

the table and draped her hand across it, displaying French-manicured nails. "I'll have a glass of sparkling wine."

The bartender served her a mini-bottle containing one glass and poured half of it in the accompanying flute for her. "Shall I put this on a tab or charge it to your room?"

"You may charge it to the house," she replied arrogantly. "My fiancé is the general manager here. I shouldn't have to pay for anything."

Lisa froze, her mind swirling at the blonde's words. *Did she just say her fiancé is the general manager of this hotel?*

Lisa's gaze dove to the blonde's left hand, the one draped over her flat purse. The woman wore an enormous diamond.

But she's so young. She can't be a day over twenty-five.

Her heart began to pound. Her mind became a jumble of confusion. Did Shawn have a fiancée or did the young woman mean Pete LaMaur—the same Pete LaMaur that had been pillow talkin' with her best friend Shakara? She only knew of one way to find out.

"Excuse me," Lisa said to her. "I couldn't help but overhear you say you're waiting for your fiancé. Would that, by any chance, be Pete LaMaur?"

The blonde gave Lisa the once over, letting Lisa know she found the intrusion of her privacy bothersome and offensive. "Excuse me?" she replied with thinly veiled disdain. "My fiancé is Shawn Wells. His family *owns* this hotel."

"Oh..." Lisa barely spoke the word. The shock had caused everything in her mind to blur.

"Is that so," the bartender said, clearly baffled that he hadn't heard of her before. "May I ask your name?"

"Brittany Stone," she said loudly, as if to establish her superiority to all within hearing distance. "Shawn and I have been engaged for six months. I flew in to surprise him."

Lisa picked up her purse and started for the door.

He's not the only one who is surprised...

"Miss... Oh, miss," the bartender called after her. "Can I get you something?"

She shook her head as she stumbled out of the lounge, her mind spinning with a sense of déjà vu.

He pursued me. He lied to me. He told me how much he loved me, but he's actually in love with a beautiful young girl...

It sounded like Rob Mancuso all over again—lies upon lies upon lies. Only this time she didn't intend to hide in the bathroom and let him simply walk away unscathed. She'd had months to think about that night and what she could have done—what she *should* have done.

She intended to find Shawn immediately. With any luck, she'd catch him with Brittany Stone. By the time she'd finished with him, he'd wish they'd never met.

****

Shawn walked into the lounge in a terrific mood. He'd just made the most important decision of his life and he couldn't wait to tell Lisa about it. On their way down the stairs to the main level, he and Pete had come up with a crazy idea for their first development project and he wanted to get her opinion.

They saw Shakara first. Her tall, willowy frame stood out in the crowd in a short, off the shoulder dress in red spandex. Her spike-heeled sandals click-clacked on the floor as she approached them. "Have you seen Lisa?"

"No," Shawn said. "Isn't she with you?"

Shakara shook her long corkscrew curls. "I told her I'd meet her here."

"Hey, babe," Pete said and wrapped his arm around her. "Can we go somewhere quiet?"

"If you see Lisa, tell her I'm waiting for her," Shawn said as Pete and Shakara left the noisy lounge to take a walk.

A young blonde sitting at a high table next to the windows turned at the sound of his voice and he found himself staring at Brittany Stone. He couldn't believe it. She'd cut her hair short so she looked different, but the same immature, inflated sense of self-importance still reflected in her eyes. He quickly glanced around to make sure Lisa hadn't picked that moment to arrive. He'd never be able to talk his way out of this disaster. "What are *you* doing here?"

Her generous smile indicated she expected him to greet her as though nothing had happened between them. In other words, as though she hadn't thrown a loud tantrum and literally tossed his engagement ring away right in front of him.

"I flew in with your father on the company jet. I've missed you, Shawn." Her full ruby lips turned down in a pout. "Aren't you glad to see me?"

"After our last episode, I never expected to see you again," he said testily and clutched her by the arm. "This is no place to discuss our personal business. We're getting out of here."

He swiftly pulled her through the lounge, ignoring the way she teetered on her flimsy, four-inch designer heels. Despite her complaints about walking too fast, he escorted her around the corner to the waiting area of the Bayside Café, now closed because of the impending storm. He didn't want Lisa to see her, talk to her or know she even existed. Brittany

Stone couldn't have picked a worse time to come strutting back into his life and he didn't want her presence to cause trouble with the woman he truly loved.

He drew in a tense breath. "What do you want, Brittany?"

"Do I have to spell it out, Shawn? The engagement is back on. I've changed my mind. I want to m-a-k-e-u-p."

She dropped her clutch on an empty chair and moved close, placing her hands on his chest. "I've been thinking, Shawn; after the wedding, I want to move to California. I told Wyn that he should turn the hotel in Los Angeles over to you to manage when it's ready to open." She gazed into his eyes as she toyed with the collar of his shirt. "I think it would be so cool to live in L. A., don't you? You could buy me a house in Malibu Beach. I'll find a new agent out there and get the caliber of modeling jobs I deserve."

Even after being apart all this time, nothing had changed with Brittany. Everything still became, in one way or another, all about her...

"For someone who said she planned to block me on her phone because I wouldn't put her first, you've certainly changed your tune." Brittany's embarrassing public breakup had infuriated him so much, he'd blocked her number, too. "Look, Brittany, I'm not moving to L.A. I'm not even coming back to the states. Go home. Go back to your glamorous life and forget about me." He pulled her hands away from his chest. His anger burst into an inferno when he saw the engagement ring glittering on her finger. "*Where did you get this?*"

She proudly held it up to the light. "Lucia gave it to me. I'm soooo happy to get it back. She found it in a sport jacket you left in the closet of your office at the Hibiscus. She was going through the pockets before sending it to the cleaners and the ring fell out. You're lucky she bothered to check! When I called her to get Wyn's unlisted cell number, she asked why I wasn't wearing it. I made up a story about accidentally leaving it on the table at our lunch date and told her I was *so* grateful to get it back."

Having more pressing matters on his mind, he'd completely forgotten about the ring. Now, he wished it had gotten lost at the cleaners. He glared at her, unmoved by her little speech. "Why aren't you listening to me? The engagement is *off*. You ended it and that's the way it's going to stay. I'm not coming back to the states with you and there is *no* chance we'll ever get back together again." He stared at her hand. "So, take the ring off and put it away." *Pawn it, for all I care.*

"What's the matter with you, Shawn?" Brittany's eyes suddenly filled with tears and she leaned against him to sob on his chest. "I love you and I know you still love me. We were meant to be together."

Denise Devine

"We were a mistake." He gently pushed her away, fed up with her carefully calculated theatrics. Instead of modeling, she should have gone to acting school. She'd have made a great villain on the silver screen. "We have nothing in common."

"We have *this*." In a dramatic show of passion, she threw her arms around him and kissed him. Irritated at her desperate attempt to manipulate him, he placed his hands on her waist intending to push her away again, but what he discovered made him pause. Her kiss did *nothing* to evoke desire within him—zilch, nada—in fact, it annoyed him and he knew she'd realized it, too.

Apart from her looks, he wondered now what he ever saw in her. Had he really been that shallow? He let go of her and stepped back. "Goodbye, Brittany. I wish only the best for you."

She pulled off the ring and threw it at him. "Get out of my way." Grabbing her purse, she stormed past him. The three-karat, white gold solitaire had bounced off his chest and dropped to the stone floor.

Shawn picked up the ring and stared at it, wishing he'd simply left it sitting in the bottom of Brittany's ice tea. He needed to find Lisa and talk to her about the situation with his ex-fiancée before she found out on her own. Otherwise, he could kiss Lisa goodbye. Literally.

Chapter Eight

LISA COULDN'T FIND Shawn anywhere. She'd taken the stairs to his office on the second-floor mezzanine and found it dark. Frustrated, she crossed the mezzanine to the parapet and looked down, searching the wide lobby for any sign of him. Had he and Brittany left the building or simply rode the elevator to his room to avoid her?

She ran part way down the stairs and looked across the lobby again. There they were, in the waiting area of the Bayside Café. Shawn stood bent over Brittany, his hands tightly circling her small waist as he kissed her.

Though a voice in her head warned her not to do it, she continued to take in the scene. His betrayal pierced her heart, bringing a rush of angry tears to her eyes. She remembered all the fun they'd had sneaking into Anna LaBore's mansion and later snooping around the Morganville Hotel. She remembered their crazy emails and the disastrous meeting at Nigel's that she *thought* had ended up bringing them closer together. Obviously, she'd been wrong. He'd simply used her as a convenient distraction...like Rob had.

By the time she reached Shawn, however, he stood alone, rubbing the back of his neck and staring at something in his palm. He looked tired and upset.

Hit him with both barrels and walk away. Don't give him the chance to try to cover up his lies with even more.

"Shawn Wells, you're a liar and a fraud," she shouted, hoping Brittany Stone had stepped into the lounge and could hear every word. "You cheated on your fiancée and you cheated on me. I hope she dumps you for what you did. As far as I'm concerned, I already have. You deserve to lose us both!"

She turned and walked away, feeling triumphant at having the last word, even though doing so had broken her heart into so many pieces it would never mend.

"Lisa, wait," he said and followed after her. "You've got this all wrong. She's really not my fiancée—"

She spun around. "Why are you bothering to hand me that lie? I met her in the lounge, Shawn. She's young. She's beautiful. And she's wearing your engagement ring."

Panic mirrored in his eyes. "Look, it's not what you think. Give me a chance to explain—"

"I saw you kissing her! That explains

Lisa: Beach Brides Series

everything."

He reached out to take her hands. "I know what it looks like to you, but please, listen to me," he argued desperately. "I don't love her, Lisa. It's over between us. I swear! It ended before I came to the island."

His clichéd attempt to lie his way out of it sickened her. She jerked from his grasp. "Get away. *You disgust me.* I never want to see you again."

Covering her ears with her hands so she couldn't hear him anymore, she ran toward the lobby as fast as she could. She had to find Shakara and tell her friend she was leaving. Pete would probably take her home, anyway.

Shakara walked in the front entrance, bawling like a baby.

What happened to her?

Lisa dashed across the room and rushed to her side. "Shakara, what's wrong?"

"I told that *bey* to leave and never come back."

"Why?" Lisa grabbed a tissue from her purse and dabbed at Shakara's tears. "What happened?"

"Don't you know? They're leaving the hotel."

Lisa blinked. "What did you say?"

"The mall project didn't get approved. Peter

said he and Shawn have lost their jobs. That means they'll be leaving the island." She sniffled and wiped her nose with the tissue. "Peter said they weren't going anywhere, but he's a liar. He'll get lonely for his family and go home. And never come back. I told him to go now and let my broken heart mend. Don't keep me hanging on."

No wonder Shawn's fiancée is here. She's come to help him pack up.

Shakara shoved her crushed tissue in her purse. "I want to leave. *Now.*"

Lisa opened the front door and stepped out into the windy night. "You're right, we need to go. There's nothing for us here."

She drove Shakara home to her apartment above her shop. On the way, she explained what happened between her and Shawn. Shakara hugged her goodbye, but had little to say, lost in her own deep unhappiness. As Lisa drove the short distance from Main Street to the B&B, her frustration broke loose and she cried aloud, letting her heart release her grief.

She pulled into the garage and shut off the car. Sitting the dim light, she wiped the tears from her face, trying to convince herself to let her sadness go. She'd left West Palm Beach to get away from hurt, deception and betrayal, but it had merely followed her to Enchanted Island.

It doesn't seem enchanted here anymore.

No more relationships for me, she vowed to herself as she freshened her face with cool liquid from her water bottle. *I'm going to concentrate on managing the B&B, like I came here to do in the first place.*

She grabbed her purse and battled the increasing wind as she ran to the house. To her surprise, the moment her hand touched the doorknob, it opened on its own. Her twenty-three-year-old niece, Bella Dubois, stood in the doorway with her hands outstretched, pulling Lisa inside.

"Gosh, the wind is getting bad," Bella said, brushing her long sand-colored hair from her round face. "Hi, cousin!"

"Hi, Bella, how long have you been here? You didn't tell us you were coming or I would have met you at the dock to help you with your suitcases."

"I got here early this morning on the ferry from Miami and spent some time visiting with my boyfriend's family before coming home," Bella said as she shut the door. "I've known James all my life, but I didn't get serious about him until we met up again in Atlanta."

Lisa gave her a hug, finding her niece's visit to be at least one bright spot in a rather dark day. "It's great to see you again. How long are you planning to stay?"

132

Denise Devine

"Oh, I'm not here for a visit." Bella's pink cheeks beamed with enthusiasm. "James and I have come back to the island permanently. When we get married, we're going to take over the B&B."

The shock hit Lisa so hard she dropped her purse. *She no longer had a job at Bella's Enchanted B&B.*

She'd always heard that lightning never struck twice in the same place—not so with bad luck. For the second time in her life, she'd lost her boyfriend and her job in one day. Now what would she do? She needed to think about her future. Where would she go from here? She had no clue. Her future looked as bleak as the hurricane charging straight toward the island.

Chapter Nine

BY SATURDAY MORNING, the hurricane had gained even more intensity and when it reached Enchanted Island, it had become a "Category 2." Winds in excess of 100 miles an hour howled across the small land mass, bending trees, spreading debris and pelting everything with driving rain.

Lisa and Elsie had spent the previous morning closing and locking the shutters to protect the windows. They'd cancelled or rescheduled all of their reservations so, except for the three women, the house stood empty.

Earlier that day, Lisa had called her parents to tell them that after the storm passed she'd be coming home for good. She promised to call them again as soon as the weather cleared to let them know she, Elsie and Bella had made it safely through the hurricane.

Internet and phone service were out by the time they awoke on Saturday morning. Soon after, the electricity went out as well, but they had large containers filled with water, battery-operated lanterns and plenty of food to see them through until the storm subsided.

Lisa moved out of her bedroom, as now it belonged to Bella, and slept upstairs in the emerald room. She wanted to be totally alone. During the night, she lay in the darkness and listened to the howling winds, wondering what to do with her life. She found herself at a crossroads and didn't know which direction to go. Getting involved with another man didn't seem to be the answer—obviously—nor did working for someone else. Her time on the island, though brief, had been a good experience. She'd learned a lot about managing a business from Elsie. Her aunt was as independent as a woman could get. Elsie's arthritis had slowed down her body, but her mind still clicked as sharp as ever.

I'm going to use everything she taught me. I'm going to stop looking to others to provide my happiness and instead make my own. It's going to be a challenge, but fun...a new adventure.

She fell asleep making a mental list of the most important things she needed to do once she got back to the states.

Once the storm passed, the women ventured outdoors to check on the damage left by the hurricane and make sure all of their neighbors were safe. The house had suffered minor damage to the roof, but the rest of the exterior had come through without any harm.

Lisa stayed on for five days to help put things

back in order. Eventually, electricity and internet were restored. As soon as her phone had coverage, she called her parents to let them know they had weathered the storm safely.

The wind damage to the roof had caused some water leakage in one of the upstairs bedrooms. Bella's boyfriend, James, came over with a couple friends who'd worked in construction, and they fixed the roof. In the meantime, Lisa helped clear all the furniture out of the bedroom that needed the walls and ceiling repaired. She also cleaned up the yard, opened all the shutters and spent a day with her best friend, Shakara.

Shakara begged Lisa to move in with her, offering to share her small apartment and teach her how to design beautiful jewelry, but Lisa declined, knowing she wouldn't be happy. She had too many memories connected with the island. Instead, she'd decided to make a fresh start somewhere new and never look back.

Several times after the storm passed, she saw the Amaryllis' managerial staff car, the Jeep Renegade, pass the house and she wondered if Shawn had left the island yet. He, Pete and Brittany Stone had most likely flown back to Florida in his father's corporate jet that same night ahead of the bad weather and by now lived far away from Enchanted Island.

On the fifth day after the storm, Lisa said

goodbye to Elsie and Bella and with suitcase in hand, walked to the waterfront to catch the ferry to Miami. Elsie hadn't wanted her to leave, but she knew the B&B didn't have enough room or a need for three managers—four once Bella got married. Besides, she'd decided on a new course for her life and couldn't wait to get started.

She arrived at the small, covered terminal fifteen minutes early to relax and enjoy the beautiful aqua hue of the Caribbean for the last time—maybe forever. Perhaps someday the hurt of Shawn's betrayal would fade away, but for now, she wanted to get far away from Enchanted Island and the pain she had encountered here.

A dockworker entered the terminal and sat down on the bench opposite her with a cup of coffee and a bag of bakery items.

"Mornin'," he said in a raspy, but cheery voice. "Ha it go?"

"I'm just fine." She smiled, feeling refreshed and invigorated. "It's a beautiful day, isn't it? The sky has never looked so blue. And you?"

"Jes' fine." He held out the paper sack. "Care for a caramel roll?"

She shook her head. "Thank you for the offer, but I've already had breakfast."

He opened the sack and pulled out a large roll dripping with a gooey caramel glaze. "You catchin' the ferry to Miami?"

She nodded. "I'm moving back to Florida to live."

"You got a new job?" He took a huge bite of his roll.

Lisa relaxed against the seat, making herself comfortable. "Well, I wouldn't call it a job because it's actually my passion, but I've decided to work for myself. I'm going to start a bed and breakfast hotel."

She hadn't planned to tell anyone just yet, but it felt terrific to say it aloud. She still had the proceeds from the sale of her townhouse and a few investments that she could cash out for a down payment on the right property. Once she found a place and started the process, she intended to send a detailed email to everyone in the book club and invite the entire group to her grand opening.

"I've got a better idea. Stay here and open a hotel with me."

That voice. It couldn't be...

She whirled around to find Shawn walking toward the terminal in a pair of worn jeans and a gray T-shirt. His thick, dark hair glistened in the bright sunlight. Her body tensed. Her heart began to pound. "W-what are you still doing on the island? I thought you'd be long gone by now..."

"I'm not going anywhere," he said boldly. "I'm

starting a new business."

She frowned. "How did you know I'd be here?"

"Shakara told me. She and Pete are back together." He approached her in the terminal, but stopped in the doorway. "Lisa, we need to talk." She started to shake her head, but he held out his hand to plead with her. "Let me tell you what I came here to say. Please, just listen."

The dockworker glanced back and forth between her and Shawn. He suddenly stood, his sober expression indicating he didn't want to intrude on their privacy. Once he left, Shawn took the man's place on the opposite bench. "I don't want you to leave."

Lisa folded her arms and stared out at the bay. "You don't have a choice in the matter."

"Look, just give me a chance to explain what really happened between me and Brittany and if it doesn't change your mind, I'll never bother you again." He gripped his knees with white-knuckled hands. "Lisa, I'm sorry for all of the hurt I've caused you and I take full responsibility for what happened that night at the Amaryllis. I didn't handle the issue with Brittany very well, but I swear, I never cheated on you or lied to you. Brittany and I broke up before I left for the island. She didn't like the idea of being stuck here without her social network and she expressed it by walking out on me."

"She still had the ring," Lisa snapped. "You were still engaged."

"When Brittany doesn't get her way, she throws things," he said and slipped his fingers into his jeans pocket, pulling out a large diamond ring. "I've been the intended target of this several times. The last time we were together before I came to the island, she threw it down and stormed out. It's a boring story, but my assistant found it and gave it back to her. That's why Brittany was wearing it when you saw her. When I met up with her in the lounge and told her I wouldn't take her back, she threw it at me."

"I saw you *kissing her*, Shawn."

He sighed. "I won't insult you by saying it didn't hold any meaning. It did. I told her to go home and forget about me. It was a kiss of goodbye."

Lisa stared at him. "Where is she now?"

"I don't know." He shrugged. "I don't care, either. She went back to Florida with my dad the same night." He scooted forward. "Lisa, I—"

"You never answered me. Why are you still here?"

His eyes twinkled. "Didn't you hear what happened?"

"I heard you lost your job because the council threw out your proposal. Other than that, no; I've been too busy cleaning up from the storm to pay attention to island gossip."

He grinned proudly. "Pete and I bought the Morganville Hotel."

Lisa gasped. "You did *what*?"

"We met with the council three days ago and laid out our plans. They bought into it. They're happy someone is reviving the place and they're backing us all the way. Not only that, but they're going to restore the cobblestone street and work with all of the merchants to improve their properties. We're going to revive downtown."

His news shocked Lisa so much, she didn't know what to say.

"I realize by the look on your face that you're still skeptical of everything I've said, but I'll prove to you that Brittany is gone from my life and she's never coming back." He held up the ring and pulled his arm back. "So long..."

"No, don't!" She lurched forward and grasped at his hand, stopping him from tossing the ring into the bay. "It's worth a lot of money! You should sell it and use the cash for the rehab of the hotel."

"Only if you agree to join forces with me and handle the finances." He dropped the ring onto her palm then closed her hand as he covered her fingers with his. "Look, I can't do this without you, Lisa. It just wouldn't be any fun." He stood, pulling her to her

Lisa: Beach Brides Series

feet. "Please stay. This project is just as important to you as it is to me and you know it." He slid his arms around her. "I need you. *I love you.*" He pulled her into his arms and kissed her deeply.

She stood in his embrace, melting under his kiss as her mind swirled with confusion. Could she open her heart to him once more?

"We'll make a dynamite team," he said as though reading her mind. "And I promise, as soon as I can get to the mainland, I'll buy you an even bigger ring."

"I'm not like Brittany," she said truthfully. "I don't care about expensive trinkets like that. I'd rather spend the money on a fantastic trip somewhere, like a hotel in the Costa Rican rainforest or exploring an ancient city like Cairo or Ephesus."

He tipped his head back and laughed, sounding relieved. "You have no idea how happy that makes me because that's what I want, too." He looked down. "Don't leave me, Lisa. Stay here and I promise you, we'll have more fun than you ever dreamed of— no matter what we're doing."

"Oh, Shawn." She laid her cheek against his chest. "That night at Nigel's, when we walked on the beach together, I knew then that I loved you more than I've ever loved anyone. That's why it hurt me so much to see you with...with her."

"I've loved you ever since that day we snuck

into the LaBore mansion," he murmured in her ear. "That's when I knew you were *the one*. You're adventurous and a little crazy, just like me."

She laughed. "I am not crazy!"

"Oh, yeah?" He hugged her tight. "I remember climbing through a bat-infested cave with you, stepping over snakes and ducking spiders as big as golf balls." He kissed her temple. "That's my kind of crazy."

The Miami-bound ferry arrived and glided alongside the dock, the blast of its horn announcing its arrival.

Shawn picked up Lisa's suitcase and grabbed her hand. "Come on. Let's go to the hotel. Let's go *home*. Pete has the electricity on and the water running now so the place is all ours. You can have any room you want, but we need to get some furniture." He grinned. "I just happen to have a key to a storeroom at the Amaryllis that is full of used stuff..."

Chapter Ten

Fourteen months later on December 29th

The bridal suite in the Morganville 1861 Hotel

"GYAL, YOUR BOONGIE looks good in that dress."

Lisa smiled at Shakara and spun around for her friend's inspection of her wedding gown, an ivory, strapless chiffon sheath with a sweetheart-shaped bodice and a nipped waist. Lisa's mother, a seamstress, had designed and stitched it.

Shakara had crafted a special bridal set for her; a simple pearl necklace with a sophisticated backdrop made of pearls, Swarovski crystal beads and a single teardrop in Tanzanite. The matching pearl earrings also each had a small Tanzanite teardrop as well.

Lisa stood in the full length cheval mirror, watching as Shakara fastened the necklace.

"You look radiant, honey." Carole Kaye stood to one side, fussing with the dress, making sure the seam lines were straight. Her dark brown hair, now peppered with gray, was twisted into a chignon at the nape of her neck.

As mother of the bride, she wore a red silk dress to coordinate with the red chiffon gowns she'd sewn for the bridal party. Lisa had chosen Shakara for her maid of honor and her two younger sisters for her bridesmaids.

A dozen women filled the bridal suite, drinking Switchta, snacking on fruit and catching up on old times as they observed the slow, painstaking process of Lisa getting ready for the family's wedding of the decade. So many friends and relatives had responded to the invitations, they had completely filled not only the Morganville Hotel, but Elsie's B&B and some of the resorts as well. All of Shawn's family that attended were staying at the Amaryllis.

Even the members of the Romantic Hearts Book Club were there—all of them. Some of the women were married now and brought their spouses.

"The wedding is starting in fifteen minutes," Carole said in a no-nonsense tone, waving her arms to shoo everyone out of the room except the bridal party.

She picked up Lisa's tulle veil with lace appliques and began to position it on her head, taking great care to get it balanced right. The local hairdresser had swept Lisa's hair into a mass of Grecian curls, interwoven with baby's breath.

"Are you nervous, honey?" Carole's hands shook as she fastened the sheer, fingertip-length garment. Until now, her mother had appeared to be in full control, ordering people around like Mother Superior, but with the wedding just minutes away, her armor had obviously begun to crack.

"No, Mom," Lisa said, turning her head. "Not at all." *How could I be nervous when the entire day has unfolded like a fairytale in a dream?*

"Stand still!"

Oops...

Lisa stood patiently, behaving like an obedient child while her mother finished positioning her veil and gave her gown one last inspection.

The door opened and Lisa's cousin, Shelby Dubois, poked her head into the room. "The musicians are ready." At Carole's nod, Shelby opened the door wide for the bridal party to exit.

Someone handed her a bouquet of red roses.

"Jeannie, Lila," Carole barked and snapped her fingers at Lisa's younger sisters, pointing to the hallway at the top of the stairs. "Line up, let's go! Shakara, you're after them."

Everyone silently did as they were told, giving each other concerned looks that said, "*What's wrong with her?*"

Carole escorted Lisa to the end of the line and

told Shelby to let the musicians know they could start the music. The bridal party descended the staircase and proceeded through the wide lobby, stopping at the back door where Lisa's father, Bob, waited to escort her into the flower-filled courtyard where the guests—and Shawn—waited.

The short, balding man smiled as they approached, but stayed silent; it was her father's way of keeping his emotions in check.

"All right," Carole said, her voice wavering as she fussed with Lisa's veil. "D-don't be nervous."

There she goes again...

"I'm fine, Mom. You'd better go and sit down. I think they're waiting for you." Lisa turned her head slowly and stared, surprised by the stricken look on Carole's face. She reached out and touched her mother's hand. "It'll be okay, Mom."

Carole's lip quivered as she grasped Lisa's fingers tightly. "I know...I just..." Her eyes began to brim with tears. "Yesterday you were my baby. Today you're getting married. The years went by so fast."

Placing a kiss on her fingertips, she reached over and touched her mother's cheek. *Mom, you look like you're at a funeral.* "Mom, you're not losing me, you're gaining a son to fuss over."

Aunt Elsie appeared and whispered a few words to Carole. Taking Carole firmly by the arm, Elsie led her to her seat in the front row.

Lisa: Beach Brides Series

The musicians, a simple duo consisting of a violin and a harp, began to play the processional for the groomsmen to start their march.

Lisa stood quietly, watching Shawn's cousin, his brother and his best friend, Pete, enter the courtyard from a side door wearing black tuxedos with white shirts. Shawn followed and took his place at the altar. He turned, waiting for Lisa to appear.

The bridal party made their way to the altar. Then the familiar cue sounded and Pachelbel's "Canon in D" began. Everyone stood and faced the bride.

Bob offered her his arm. "Are you ready?"

She nodded and slipped her arm in his. "Let's go, Dad."

With her father smiling proudly at her side, Lisa stepped into the courtyard and began her walk, barely aware of the sea of smiling faces doting upon her. All she could see was Shawn and the love gleaming in his eyes. She made her way to the altar and took her place beside him.

Bob lifted her veil and kissed her cheek. "I love you, sweetheart," he whispered. He stared at Shawn. "Take good care of my little girl."

"Yes, sir."

Shawn nodded respectfully as Bob stepped away, but his gaze centered on Lisa. "We're leaving first thing in the morning for Egypt, *Island Girl*," he whispered and motioned toward the inside breast pocket of his coat. "I've got the plane tickets right here."

Lisa smiled. "Great, *City Boy*. I can't wait!"

The minister cleared his throat and stepped toward them. "Dearly beloved..."

A fairytale wedding, a honeymoon in a historic hunting lodge formerly owned by an Egyptian prince and ten days of exploring the wonders of the ancient world with her "dream hero."

Life couldn't get much better than that.

Author Bio

Denise Devine is a USA TODAY bestselling author who has had a passion for books since the second grade when she discovered Little House on the Prairie by Laura Ingalls Wilder. She wrote her first book, a mystery, at age thirteen and has been writing ever since. If you'd like to know more about her, you can visit her at www.deniseannettedevine.com.

BEACH BRIDES THANK YOU!

Thanks for reading Lisa's story.

Hope's book is next.

Read a Sneak Peek in the Excerpt.

Meet all of the Beach Brides!

Meg (Julie Jarnagin)

Tara (Ginny Baird)

Denise Devine

Nina (Stacey Joy Netzel)

Clair (Grace Greene)

Jenny (Melissa McClone)

Lisa (Denise Devine)

Hope (Aileen Fish)

Kim (Magdalena Scott)

Rose (Shanna Hatfield)

Lily (Ciara Knight)

Faith (Helen Scott Taylor)

Amy (Raine English)

Excerpt Copyright Information

Prologue and Chapter One from *Hope (Beach Brides Series)* by Aileen Fish

Hope

Beach Brides Series

by

Aileen Fish

Prologue

HOPE'S MESSAGE IN a bottle:

Dear Sir Galahad,

Once upon a time I believed in fairy tale endings, and I think a part of me still does. What I don't believe in is a knight on a white horse riding into my life and making everything perfect. Rather ironic, isn't it, since I call you Sir Galahad? For the sake of the game, I guess what I want is a man who'll not give up, who'll stick it out until the end, even when the setbacks seem overwhelming. Life isn't easy, but it's so worth it!

Since this bottle will end up twenty thousand leagues under water somewhere around Atlantis, I'm safe in pretending the good parts of fairy tales are true. Life is happy day to day, and who wants an ending?

Thanks for listening—er, reading. Maybe we'll meet one night in our dreams.

alwayshopeful@...

Chapter One

STANDING IN THE principal's office of Lane Elementary School happened much too often lately. Hope Reynolds kept her gaze on the children outside, who ran screaming and playing in the weak winter sunshine.

"I know you'd hoped counseling would help Jayden, but we need to do something in the meantime," Principal Joe Jennings said. "This is the third time he's started a fight this month."

Turning away from the window, Hope rubbed her arms to ward off the chill the situation gave her. "I'm at wit's end. I don't know what to do anymore."

"I have to suspend him, or it will look like favoritism." Joe's lips were thin, but she knew his distress was more at the situation than Jayden.

"I understand." Hopefully her mom would understand, too. She felt Hope treated her son with kid gloves, and would happily use a firmer hand to his backside, which Hope was firmly against. The problem was, Mom was the only person Hope could ask to babysit. "I'll let Marni know she's on her own for the rest of the day, and then take him home."

Returning to the school library, Hope found her friend and coworker Marni. "He's at it again."

Marni looked up from the cart full of books she was shelving. "Oh no."

"He's suspended for a week. I hope Mom doesn't have plans.

Her son Jayden hadn't taken Hope's divorce well when he was three, and when her long-time boyfriend moved out six months ago, Jayden's angry outbursts multiplied. If she wasn't the head librarian at Lane, he would likely have been expelled.

"Have you had any luck convincing your ex-husband to let Jayden visit?" Marni slid a book between two others on the shelf.

Folding her arms across her breasts, Hope shook her head. "You're kidding, right? With his new wife and baby, he has no interest in us."

"Jayden needs a man in his life. What about sports? Sign-ups for soccer are still open."

"I don't know...he might just learn to kick in addition to hitting."

"You need to find a good guy. You both can use it." Biting back a grin, Marni looked away.

"Look what happened when the last one left. If I date at all, I'm not going to let Jayden meet the guy. He feels abandoned when I break up with someone. I won't subject him to a revolving door of men. We'll get through this, somehow."

She really didn't mind being alone, most of the time. Her girlfriends were there for a movie night or going out dancing. Valentine's Day without a date didn't faze her, and her mom made sure her birthday didn't go unnoticed. And Jayden filled every free moment with his love. Life was good.

Hope picked up her purse and coat and returned to the front office to find her son so they could go home. The weather was perfect for hot cocoa and cookies, but Jayden might take that as a reward for misbehaving. He'd have his usual apple slices and milk, then do his homework, and she'd insist no playing video games for a few days. Mom would have to suffer through the extra grumpiness of a whiny eight-year-old.

Her week ahead stretched for miles in front of her, even though she'd only be with her son in the evening after work. She'd spend her lunch break making calls to the counselor for a referral for someone to help. She had to find a way to help him release his anger in a safe way before someone got seriously hurt.

****

Chase Bowman tossed another bale of hay onto his flatbed truck. The weather had been unusually cold and his supply was getting low. With more snow on the ground than in past winters, there was nothing for his cattle to eat other than the hay he threw down daily, but they were fat and healthy, which was all he could ask. "That's it for here. Let's take the rest to the southwest corner in case any strays are down there."

"Sounds good." Matt Frost, his best friend and ranch hand, climbed into the truck.

The quarter-mile ride was spent in silence, but as soon as they exited the warm cab, Matt started in on his current obsession. "Have you written her?"

Slanting him a grimace, Chase simply said, "No."

"How long have you had that bottle? Six months? A year?"

He knew exactly how long it had been since he found the bottle in the sand when he and Dad had gone fishing for the last time off Matagorda Bay. Three weeks after they'd returned to the ranch, Dad lost his battle with cancer. That was exactly five months, two weeks and three days ago.

Chase would have never imagined how sharply he'd feel his father's loss. The days of the two of them riding the land were long gone, but sitting across the table from an empty chair sucked. Mom was quieter now, still deep in her grieving. The house had a pallor, which he was all too happy to escape each morning.

"Ten years from now the answer will be the same. No, I haven't emailed her. She's probably a scammer, some guy planning to ask for money to come to America. I'm not wasting my time."

"Then why do you still have the bottle?"

Shoot, he needed to toss that thing. He wouldn't even have the bottle if it weren't for Dad. Now it was a memento of their final vacation together. It had sat on the windowsill in the tack room, forgotten, until Matt noticed it and read the letter. "I guess I was too lazy to recycle it."

"Uh-huh. You put the letter back inside, I noticed. You're planning to get in touch. You should. You could use some female company."

"Email isn't company, and didn't cyber-sex go out in the nineties?" After tossing the last bale, Chase took off his gloves and tucked them part way into his pocket. "It ain't happening, Matt. You're wasting your time."

He had no valid reason for hanging onto the message in the bottle. Still, something in the short note drew him to the woman who wrote it. She allowed herself to dream, but recognized them for what they were. Fiction. She appreciated her life as it was, just like he did. What could it hurt to write her? Winter nights were long and he could use a distraction from TV. He didn't believe in fairy tales, either, but it'd be a kick to see what response he got.

What the heck...might as well do it.

****

After finishing the weekly accounting paperwork, Chase stared at the blank email on the computer monitor. This had to be one of his stupider ideas. He was likely to take as long composing the letter as he had getting to this point.

Taking a cue from her message, he began.

Dear Hopeful,

Geez, that sounded like a reply to a personals ad. But what else could he call her?

First let me say my horse is black, not white, and I don't have armor.

Mom insisted he hid his heart behind an armor shield, but that was an exaggeration.

Your message intrigues me. You sound as happy as you say you are, so why did you write a letter like this? I guess it's the same reason as mine— curiosity.

Since you took the time to toss a bottle into the ocean and you included an email address, I guess you're wondering where it ended up. I found it in the Gulf of Mexico and brought it home to central California. If we were speaking in person, I'd ask where you threw it. Then we might talk about where we live, or whether we were on vacation or walking a beach near home. After a brief, polite conversation we'd part ways and go on with our lives, taking a bit of fairy tale magic with us.

But since we're communicating electronically, we can skip all that and get back to the daily grind. I hope your day went well, and your life continues to be happy. As a dreamer and a realist, I have a feeling you'll make sure it is.

SirGalahad@...

*** End of Excerpt ***

Hope

Beach Brides Series

By

Aileen Fish

Made in the USA
Columbia, SC
17 March 2019